MW01026893

A
Goose Creek
CHRISTMAS

VIRGINIA SMITH

Angela —
Merry Christmas
Virginia Smith

N$B

Next Step Books
P.O. Box 70271
West Valley City, UT 84170

This is a work of fiction. Names, characters, places, and incidents are products of the author's imagination or are used fictitiously. Any resemblance to actual persons, living or dead, is entirely coincidental.

A GOOSE CREEK CHRISTMAS
Copyright © 2016 by Virginia Smith

eBook Published by Harvest House Publishers
Eugene, Oregon 97402
www.harvesthousepublishers.com
ISBN 978-0-7369-6878-2 (eBook)

Print Book Published by Next Step Books
P.O. Box 70271, West Valley City, Utah 84170
www.NextStepBooks.org
ISBN 978-1-937671-37-2 (Print Book)

Cover by Katie Brady Design

All rights reserved. No part of this publication may be reproduced, stored in a retrieval system, distributed, or transmitted in any form or by any means—electronic, mechanical, digital, photocopy, recording, or any other—without the prior written permission of the publisher. Participation in or encouragement of piracy of copyrighted materials in violation of author's and publisher's rights is strictly prohibited.

For my family,
who fills every Christmas with love and laughter.

Chapter One

Y ou're firing me?" Al rocked backward in the chair.

The human resources manager folded her hands and rested them on top of the papers scattered across the surface of her desk. "We're not firing you, Mr. Richardson. We're offering you an early retirement package."

"But I'm not supposed to retire for another year and a half." One year, five months, and nineteen days to be exact. He had a countdown going on his computer.

From the chair beside him, Al's boss reached over and slapped him on the back. "So you get out a year and a half early, dude. Congratulations!"

Though Al always attempted to hide his dislike for the young man who'd been hired to take the management position when his former boss resigned, today he did not feel up to the task. How could he treat a manager who referred to his employees as "dude" with anything but disdain?

"I'm not serving a prison sentence," he informed Josh Lewis in a chilly tone. "I enjoy my job at J&J Services. I'm not ready to leave it yet."

The young man cast a pained glance toward the HR lady.

She tapped a manicured fingernail on the stack of papers. "I assure you, this is a very generous offer. Two weeks' severance for each year of service, and we're extending your termination date until your actual retirement would have taken place. At that time you'll be fully vested in your pension plan. You'll continue to receive employee benefits until that date, including medical and life insurance for you and" — she glanced down — "Mildred."

Millie. The mention of his wife's name served as a sobering reminder. They had plans. He had responsibilities. If he lost his job, their timeline would be ruined.

She'd insist on opening that blasted B&B early!

The HR lady continued. "Since you will have been here thirty years on your retirement date, that's sixty weeks of severance. You can opt to continue to receive it as a biweekly paycheck or in a lump sum."

Lewis gave a low whistle. "Dude, that's a boatload of money. You'll be rich."

Al did a quick mental calculation. "I have more than seventy-five weeks until retirement. If I take this package, I'll lose money."

The HR lady's eyes flickered sideways to exchange another glance with Lewis before looking back at him. "That's a valid concern, and a point we're prepared to negotiate. I'll need to get the vice president's approval, but I think he'll agree to increase your severance package to cover any loss of income."

Dumfounded, Al could only stare at the

woman. Did they want to be rid of him that badly?

He twisted in his chair to face his boss. "But why? I'm a good programmer. Nobody knows that system like I do. I installed the thing. I know every line of code in every program. I've kept it purring like a cat for the past decade."

"That dinosaur?" The young man crossed one leg over the other and wrapped his hands around his knee, his foot swinging in the air. "The technology is antiquated. We're ripping it out and installing new software. You know. Out with the old, in with the new."

"Uh..." Alarm colored the HR lady's features. "He's referring to the computer system, of course. This decision is based on our need for a different skill set. We must bring people onboard who have experience with the new software. I assure you, Mr. Richardson, that your age is not a consideration."

Right. Al almost snorted. She had to say that to protect the company against an age discrimination lawsuit. Since Lewis's arrival three months ago, he'd buddied up with the younger programmers, including them in meetings Al was not invited to, taking them out to lunch while Al sat at his desk and ate his daily sandwich. Lewis had even included the annoying

Franklin Thacker in his—

He stiffened. Narrowing his eyes, he allowed suspicion to creep into his voice. "Who else are you firing?"

"Nobody," Lewis replied at the same time the HR lady said, "That's confidential information." She turned a disgusted look on the young man.

Al ignored her and fixed a stare on his boss. "You're keeping everyone except me? Even Thacker?"

With an exaggerated sigh, Lewis uncrossed his legs and swiveled his chair until he faced Al directly. "Look, dude, it's nothing personal. The fact is, you've been here so long you're the highest-paid employee on the team. I can hire two top-notch programmers who have the skills we need for less than we're paying you."

"Mr. Richardson." The human resource manager forced him to look at her. "We want you to know we value the contribution you've made to J&J over the years. This action has nothing to do with your performance, which has been exemplary. It's strictly a business decision. We've examined every alternative, and we believe this solution is fair to everyone involved."

Fair? How could being let go five weeks before Christmas, destroying a man's future, possibly be considered fair?

He folded his arms across his chest. "What if I refuse?"

Judging by the glance the two exchanged, they'd discussed the possibility.

She leaned back in her chair. "That is your decision, of course. We can't force you to agree. But I feel it only fair to advise you that if you turn down this offer, the company will consider other means to fund the new software project we're committed to, including a mandatory reduction in force."

A layoff. And from the look on her face, Al would probably be the only one laid off.

"I assure you, Mr. Richardson, this offer" — she rested her hand on the papers in front of her—"is far more generous than our traditional severance package."

The inevitable loomed like a cloud over his head. He was being ousted, and there was nothing he could do about it.

The stiffness in his spine collapsed, and he slumped forward. "How long do I have?"

He pretended not to see the grin of triumph that split Lewis's face.

At least the lady spoke with a note of compassion in her voice. "In cases like this, when an employee has access to classified information, the separation occurs immediately. I'll escort you to your cubicle and remain with you while you clean out your belongings." She paused. "It's not personal, I promise. It's company policy."

Through a fog of misery, Al understood the reasoning. If he were the vindictive sort, he could sign on to his computer and do real damage to J&J's systems while they weren't looking. Surely they didn't think him capable of that.

"Not only that, but we're gonna throw you a retirement party. The whole team will be there." Lewis sounded positively cheerful as he gave Al a chummy slap on the shoulder. "You pick the time and place. Any day next week except Tuesday works for me."

For a moment Al battled to hold his tongue in check. How he'd love to tell this young jerk a thing or two. Instead, he pointedly ignored the offer of a party and held the gaze of the HR lady. With as much dignity as he could muster, he asked, "Where do I sign?"

"We *always* put the decorations up the day after Thanksgiving. It's a tradition." Millie picked up her coffee mug and, with a delicate pinkie extended, took a tiny sip while watching Lulu over the rim.

They sat at Millie's kitchen table enjoying their usual Friday morning ritual of coffee and muffins. For Thursday afternoon tea, Millie and her best friend, Violet, occupied the Victorian-era house's opulently decorated dining room with gleaming silver trays and bone china tea-cups. Friday mornings were different. The elegance would be lost on Lulu, who was more of a kitchen sort of friend.

Lulu dismissed Millie's explanation by blowing a raspberry between her large, orange-tinted lips. "That's not a good reason. Frankie and I put up our tree at the beginning of November. Walmart started puttin' out their Christmas stuff before Halloween, and the radio's been playing festive songs for weeks."

Millie indulged in an expansive shudder. "Which I switch off immediately. It's ridiculous to rush the holiday like that. Thanksgiving gets lost in the shuffle, buried beneath a mountain of blinking lights and glittering garland."

"If we start this weekend, that's less than a

week early. Nobody's gonna get upset over a few days."

Millie set her mug on the table and caught Lulu's eye in a direct gaze. "When you became Goose Creek's Main Street Manager you asked me to guide you in the town's expectations, remember? Trust me on this. If you try to decorate Main Street before Thanksgiving, you'll alienate people." She paused to give her next argument the emphasis it deserved. "Frieda will be furious."

At the mention of the formidable owner of the Freckled Frog Consignment Shop, Lulu visibly cowed. She sank back in her chair, eyes wide. The two had already battled over the placement of the mum planters for the Fall Festival, and Lulu had been forced to concede defeat when Frieda threatened to circulate a petition among the town's business owners. Tradition held then, as Millie had no doubt it would in the matter of the Christmas decorations.

Lulu pawed through the basket of muffins and selected one on the bottom. Suppressing another shudder, Millie sipped again from her coffee mug as her friend split open the steaming pastry and slathered butter on both sides.

"I guess I can wait till next week." She popped half a muffin in her mouth at once.

Talking around it, she said, "But those mums are starting to look bad. I hate having our town looking scruffy with dead flowers all up and down Main Street."

Millie averted her eyes from the view of masticated muffin in her friend's mouth. Lulu had asked her to advise on matters regarding Goose Creek. Table manners were not part of the arrangement, though at times Millie was forced to clamp her teeth to refrain from delivering a gentle reminder, such as she would give her grandchildren.

At the thought of grandchildren, a familiar prickle stung her eyes. Christmas was her favorite time of year, and this year's celebration would be extra special, because now they had a grand home with enough bedrooms for everyone. But she was having trouble mustering her normal enthusiasm. How could they celebrate a Richardson family Christmas without the *whole* family being present? Alison and her husband, Nick, who was stationed in Italy, had informed them that they would not be able to make the trip this year. Worse, their baby, Melody, would have her two-month checkup next week. How was it possible that Millie had a granddaughter she'd never met? It was a tragedy, that's what it was.

"What's wrong with you?"

Millie looked up from her plate to find Lulu peering at her beneath a heavily creased brow.

"Nothing." She forced a brave smile and banished the tears.

"Doesn't look like nothing from here." Her friend's eyelids, to which a thick coat of bright blue color had been applied, narrowed. "*Nothing* doesn't make people cry, and you have the looks of a gal who's getting ready to blubber."

"I was just thinking of little Melody." Millie could not hold back a sniffle. "She's growing up without me."

Compassion settled on the narrow face across the table, an expression that did not often appear on Lulu Thacker's horse-like features. "I don't understand why you don't hop on a plane and zip over there. If I was lucky enough to have a grandkid, nothing would keep me away."

The idea had definitely occurred to Millie, and she'd gone so far as to investigate airfare. Albert had flushed purple when she told him the price.

"We don't have that kind of money lying around," he'd said. "We've already decimated our savings remodeling this house."

The reminder stung, especially because he

never missed the opportunity to bring up the escalating cost of the B&B's renovations. Besides, Millie suspected the primary reason for his refusal lay in an unreasonable fear of flying, which he refused to admit. She had almost suggested that she go alone, but somehow could not muster the courage. Albert would have been offended at the suggestion that she visit his darling daughter without him.

Millie picked up her napkin and dabbed at a drop of coffee on the vinyl placemat. "It isn't feasible right now. Besides, Nick's overseas tour ends next summer, and we're hoping he'll get stationed in Kentucky—at Fort Campbell or Fort Knox. Then they'll be as close as our other children."

"At least you'll see that young'un before her first birthday." The second half of the muffin disappeared behind Lulu's oversized front teeth, and she washed it down with a loud slurp of coffee. "Now, about the decorations. I think we need something new this year. Those lighted wreaths are old fashioned, and the bows are so faded they're closer to pink than red."

Millie allowed herself to be distracted from her gloomy thoughts. "I like the vintage Christmas look. It says something about Goose Creek's long history." When Lulu would have interrupted, she rushed on. "You're right about the bows, though. They probably are showing their age. I'm sure it won't cost much to make new ones."

"Why waste good money trying to spiff up something that'll probably fall apart in another year or two anyway? What we need is a different look."

"What did you have in mind?" Millie asked the question almost fearfully. She'd been inside Lulu's house often enough to know decorating was not the woman's strong point. The Thackers had purchased the house from Millie and Al and then proceeded to change practically everything. Their right, of course, but the alterations were painful to see. The family room, which paid tribute to the Louisville Cardinals, bore bright red walls, a red sofa, matching recliners, and crimson curtains. Somewhere she'd found a carpet the exact same hue as the walls, which gave the odd impression of being inside an upside-down scarlet tunnel. The room left Millie feeling like Alice in Wonderland every time she visited. She half expected to be served tea on the ceiling.

Albert, a die-hard Kentucky Wildcat fan, refused to visit Franklin and Lulu's home. He claimed he couldn't bear to see the house where he'd built and raised his family being infested—his word—by Thackers, but Millie wondered if he'd taken offense at her description of *his* favorite room paying constant tribute to a rival team. Anyone who knew Albert knew one did not mess with his two sports passions—Purdue out of school loyalty, and the University of Kentucky because he'd caught the local fanaticism when they moved to Goose Creek several decades before. Not to say there weren't Louisville fans in Goose Creek, but they kept a low profile, especially during basketball season.

All except Franklin, of course, who did not understand the meaning of subtlety.

Lulu took a final slurp of coffee, set her mug down, and leaned over it. "I've been searching on the Internet. Instead of those old wreaths on the streetlights, what do you think about geese made out of green and red tinsel? I found a place that'll make 'em for us cheap, and they'll even put blinking lights all over 'em. I figure we could hang them so they look like they're flying up the east side of the railroad tracks toward the big Christmas tree, and down the west side like they just left there."

Try though she might, Millie could not envision anything remotely festive about red and green blinking geese flying from the light posts up and down Main Street.

Lulu cocked her head sideways. "Don't grab ya, huh? Then what about some of those blinking light sculptures like they have over at the Kentucky Horse Park? You know, the kind that look as if they're moving, only it's lights turning off and on? There's all kinds to choose from. I saw one that had Santa sitting on a motorcycle, and it looked like his wheels were really turning." Her eyes lit, and she waved a hand across the table. "Oh! Oh! And there's one that's a big frog all made up of green lights, and there's a fly above his head, and suddenly pink lights that look like a tongue shoot out of the frog's mouth and snatch that fly, and then the frog chews it up." Grinning, she leaned back. "I know Frieda would love that one mounted up on the roof of the Freckled Frog."

Millie could not fathom Frieda's reaction to such a suggestion. "Aren't those lighted sculptures expensive?"

Lulu dismissed the question with a shrug. "You'd be surprised the bargains you can find on the Internet. I've bookmarked several folks who're selling them. Why, there was this guy down in South Carolina who set up a ton of the things in his yard every year, and he died. His kids want to get rid of them, and they're going cheap. They even have one that's a flock of ducks taking off flying, and all of a sudden a man in camouflage hops up and blasts 'em out of the air."

While Lulu indulged in one of her loud guffaws, Millie clenched her teeth. Dead ducks up and down Goose Creek's Main Street were even worse than tinsel geese. It would give the children nightmares. In fact, it would give *her* nightmares.

Her coffee mug empty, she stood and gathered her dishes. "You may receive some pushback from the more traditional residents and business owners. They prefer the quaint, subdued seasonal trimmings. Gold and silver wreaths with white lights, and of course the Christmas tree at the south end of Main. All the stores put up gold and silver with white lights in their front windows. It gives Goose Creek a charming, small-town appearance. Besides, it's a little late to buy new decorations now, isn't it?"

"Nope. My honey bun and I can zip down to South Carolina and get 'em tomorrow."

Millie swallowed an exasperated sigh. "If you replace the bows on the wreaths, everyone will be happy."

Judging by the scowl on Lulu's face, she did

not agree. Orange lips tightened and twisted, while her brows drew together in thought. "Somebody's gonna snap those babies up quick. I think Frankie and I will go get 'em tomorrow, just so nobody else does."

"But you don't have a budget for something like that." Millie adopted a stern tone. "The city council will probably pay for new bows, but they certainly won't pay for light sculptures."

"I told you, they're selling for cheap. I'll pay for them. Frankie won't mind. Then I'll show 'em around so's folks can get an idea of what I'm talking about."

The business owners along Main Street would put Lulu straight in no time. Lucy Cardwell would certainly not relish the idea of looking out the drugstore's front window to see a fly-munching frog atop Frieda's store across the street. And what Tuesday Love, nature-lover that she was, would say about dead ducks falling from the sky, Millie could only guess.

"I'm afraid you'll be wasting your money."

Lulu dismissed the comment with a wave. "If people don't like 'em, we'll put 'em up in our yard. My honey bun's been saying he wants to dress the place up for Christmas."

Poor Violet, who lived next door to the Thackers, would not appreciate the display any more than Goose Creek's business owners. Millie set the dishes in the sink and then retrieved the muffins.

Lulu stretched her long neck to eye the basket as it left the table. "Mind if I take a couple home? Frankie loves apple cinnamon."

The memory of Lulu digging through the basket, touching every muffin in her effort to retrieve a hot one from the bottom, came to mind. Though Lulu was certainly a cleaner housekeeper than Violet, Millie had spied a bit of dirt beneath two of those chewed fingernails. She smiled at her guest. "You may take them all. Albert prefers blueberry."

Albert would devour any muffin she made, but at least the baked goods wouldn't end up in the garbage bin.

Millie's Apple Cinnamon Muffins

2 cups all-purpose flour
¾ cup light brown sugar
1 tsp. baking soda
½ tsp. salt
2 tsp. cinnamon
¼ tsp. nutmeg
1 cup buttermilk *or* canned coconut milk
1 T. canola oil
3 T. unsweetened, natural applesauce
1 large egg
1 tsp. vanilla extract
2 cups peeled apples, diced

Topping
½ cup brown sugar
2 T. all-purpose flour
1 tsp. cinnamon
¾ cup old-fashioned oats
3 T. butter, room temperature

½ cup nuts, finely chopped (op-
tional)

Preheat oven to 375°. Spray muffin
tins (18 regular size or 12 large size)
with cooking spray or line with paper
cupcake liners.

In a large bowl, combine the flour,
brown sugar, baking soda, salt, cinnamon, and nutmeg. In a second
bowl, stir together the buttermilk or coconut milk, oil, applesauce, egg, and
vanilla extract. Pour the wet ingredients over the dry ingredients and mix
until combined. Do not overmix. Fold
in the diced apples.

For the topping, combine brown sugar,
flour, cinnamon, and oats. Cut in the
butter. Add the nuts, if desired, and
combine with a fork until crumbly.

Fill each muffin cup three-fourths full
with batter and then sprinkle with the
topping. Bake for 20 minutes or until
muffins are browned and a toothpick
inserted in the center of a muffin
comes out clean. Let muffins cool for

10 minutes before removing from tins. Makes 18 regular size or 1 dozen large muffins.

Chapter Two

The half-filled cardboard box on the passen-
ger seat burned like an ember in Al's pe-
ripheral vision. This was all he had to show for
nearly three decades of service? A framed picture of Millie taken fifteen years ago. A stack of

snapshots of the kids and grandkids he'd tacked to the wall of his cubicle above his computer monitor. The magnetized paper clip holder one of the boys had given him for a long-ago Christmas. A few file folders with personal papers inside, which his human resource escort had examined while he stood watching and feeling like a criminal accused of stealing corporate secrets. His nameplate, of course, since soon his cubicle would be occupied by someone else.

Someone younger.

His hands clenched the steering wheel. Should he hire an attorney? Claim age discrimination? He probably had a good case. A wave of retribution swelled in his chest and then receded like the tide washing back out to sea. What good would a lawsuit do? Cases like that were expensive. The lawyers would take a chunk of any settlement he might get, and he'd end up with less than the severance package they'd given him. And probably forfeit his retiree insurance in the process.

A car's horn dragged him out of his gloomy thoughts. The traffic light in front of him glowed green. With an apologetic wave at the impatient man behind him, Al stepped on the gas pedal. The Ford pickup pulled into the left lane and sped around him, the driver tossing a glare his way as he passed.

He directed an excuse toward the truck's rear bumper. "Gimme a break, will you? I'm old and unemployed."

How would Millie take the news? He dismissed the question the moment it entered his mind. He knew exactly how his wife of nearly forty years would react. She would be taken by surprise, as he had been, but would recover quickly. Given Millie's naturally cheerful nature, she'd put a positive spin on this devastating blow within a minute or two. *We'll have time to travel*, she would say. *We can finally use your motorhome and go see the Grand Canyon.* That, of course, would only be for his benefit, an attempt to cheer him up. Eventually she would get around to the point he dreaded hearing. *We can open the B&B early, get some paying guests, and begin building up our savings again.*

A shudder shook his frame. Last spring they had entertained a few experimental guests, a sort of practice run she'd called it. The results had been disastrous. Three weeks of misery, and in the end not a single penny's profit. No. He couldn't face that again, not yet. Not while he was still reeling at being sledgehammered, forced out to pasture before his time. Depression already dragged at him like a millstone

24

necklace. He wouldn't be able to come up with a single plausible excuse in the face of his wife's cheerful insistence that they hang out their shingle and start taking reservations.

Another traffic light turned yellow up ahead, and he slowed to a stop. The B&B was Millie's dream, her endeavor. Knowing his capable wife, she would make a success of it. In no time, his home would have a constant stream of strangers in and out, and Millie would be in her element, cooking delectable breakfasts and making sure every bedroom had fresh flowers. She'd probably put mints on their pillows at night. And what would become of him? He'd be reduced to carrying luggage, waiting tables, and performing whatever menial tasks she came up with. His wife would become his boss.

Unthinkable. The man was supposed to be the breadwinner. That was the natural order of things.

The obvious answer struck him. He wouldn't tell her. Not for a while, anyway. Not until he had time to think and come up with a plan of his own. Straightening his shoulders, Al let the idea settle. Yes, that was the answer, at least in the short term. He wouldn't actually lie, just withhold the news for a while. Only long enough to figure out his next move.

After the decision was made, a sort of peace settled over him. At home the routine would not change. He'd still get up, dress in his work clothes, and leave the house at seven fifteen as always. During the day he'd have plenty of time to figure out an arrangement he could live with. Next week was a short week because of Thanksgiving, so it would only be for a few days. It was a good plan.

The traffic light changed, and with a lighter heart he started through the intersection. Then a thought slapped him like a blow to the head.

Franklin Thacker.

He slammed on the brakes, earning another angry honk from the car behind him. Thacker occupied the cubicle next to his at work and lived in Goose Creek. A thoroughly insufferable man, but his wife and Millie were friends.

Jerking the turn signal on, he executed a quick right turn and then steered his vehicle into the closest parking lot. A quick rummage through his box of belongings produced his cell phone, which he flipped open and turned on. Agonizing moments passed as the ancient device powered up. Millie frequently accused him of owning the only workable flip phone still in existence, but why spend money for a fancy one as long as this one still did the job? Finally, he was able to punch in a phone number.

"Goooooood morning. Franklin Thacker here."

The sing-song tone set Al's teeth on edge, but he didn't waste time. "Thacker, it's me."

"Bert?" The man's voice lowered to a whisper. "Oh, man, I just heard. What a shocker. Everybody's talking about it. I can't believe they'd fire an old guy like you who's been here a hundred years."

Al ground his teeth. How old did Thacker think he was, anyway? "Twenty-eight years."

He'd been thankful that Lewis had called a department meeting while he cleaned out his cubicle. At least he hadn't been subjected to the stares and whispers of his coworkers. Though he would love to question Thacker further and find out exactly what was said about his departure, he had no time to waste.

"You haven't called Lulu yet, have you?" Al directed a mental plea toward heaven and held his breath as he awaited the answer.

"I was getting ready to when you called. We just got back to our desks."

Thank goodness.

"Look, I need you to do something for me." Al swallowed hard. How it galled to ask Thacker for a favor.

A pause on the line, and Thacker's whisper became conspiratorial. "Is it illegal?"

Al pulled the phone away from his ear to give it a disgusted look before responding. "Of course not! I need you to keep this under your hat for a while. Don't tell Lulu or anyone else in Goose Creek."

An even shorter pause, and then, "Not gonna tell the missus, huh?"

One thing about Thacker. The man was irritating in the extreme, but he was quick on the uptake.

"No, I'm not." Feeling guilty, Al rushed on. "Not immediately, anyway. I need a while to settle some things. I want to have a plan in place. I have a few ideas I'd like to nail down first."

A complete lie, but a necessary one. Necessary for his self-esteem, that is.

"Weeeeelll." Thacker stretched the word into three syllables. "I have a hard time keeping secrets from Sugar Lips. All she has to do is give me *that look,* and I melt like ice cream in July. That woman's got feminine wiles oozing out of her pores. You know what I'm talking about, dontcha? I mean, you're old and all, but surely you still—"

"I know the look," Al hurried to say, repugnance settling in his stomach. "But if you don't tell Lulu you're keeping a secret, she'll have no reason to try her"—he swallowed hard—"feminine wiles on you."

"Good point. Okay, buddy. Us Geese gotta stick together, right? My lips are sealed. I mean, my beak is sealed." Thacker's trademark guffaw blasted through the phone, ending in a grating snort.

Even so, Al let out a pent-up breath. "I appreciate it."

"No problemo, amigo." His voice lost all trace of its customary bluster. "Listen, Al, if you need anything, I'm here for you."

A lump formed in Al's throat, and he had a hard time getting an answer out. "Thanks, Franklin."

He hung up and sat staring at his phone. For the first time in all the years they'd known each other, Thacker had called him Al instead of Bert. If his annoying former coworker felt it appropriate to drop the irritating nickname he knew Al hated, his situation *must* be as pathetic as he thought.

"That's the last one, Mrs. Smellenberg. All vaccinated and ready to go." Susan placed the fifth kitten back in the pet carrier and latched the door. "Have you found homes for them?"

"Only three." The woman's expression became hopeful. "You don't happen to know anyone who wants a six-toed kitten, do you?"

"No, but you're welcome to put a notice on the bulletin board in our waiting room." Susan noted the date and treatment code in the file folder. "Tuesday Love might also let you hang a sign in the window of the Day Spa. She's extremely sympathetic to polydactyl cat owners."

Mrs. Smellenberg brightened. "That's a good idea. Is there anything special I need to do for Taffy?"

Susan peered into the second carrier, where the kittens' newly spayed mama lay dozing. "She's going to be groggy for several hours, so give her a quiet place to rest. It's best to keep the kittens and your children away from her for a day or two. Some cats get cranky as the anesthetic wears off. I'll give you some pain pills and a bag of special litter to use for the next week, until that incision heals."

"I wish I'd had her spayed *before* she got pregnant. But since she's an inside cat, I thought I had time." Picking up the kittens' carrier, the woman heaved a sigh. "She only got out of the house once, but that was enough."

With a sympathetic smile, Susan lifted Taffy's crate and followed her owner out to the reception area. Her next patient, a brindle-and-white pit bull, strained at the leash in the Playful Pups waiting room, its black nose quivering in their direction.

She handed Taffy's file folder to Alice. "Take twenty percent off the vaccination total." She smiled at Mrs. Smellenberg. "A volume discount."

"Thank you, Dr. Susan." The woman dug in her purse and produced a credit card.

Alice took it, and, when she turned in the reception chair to run it through the machine, dropped it on the floor.

"Clumsy me," she mumbled, a pink stain rising in her cheeks. She retrieved the card, punched the total into the reader, and swiped. While she waited for the receipt to print, her gaze flickered toward the waiting room, and the blush deepened.

Curious, Susan glanced in that direction. The man holding the other end of the pit's leash stared at them, a shy smile playing around his lips. Correction. His stare was fixed on Alice.

The receptionist tore off the receipt and

placed it on the counter for Mrs. Smellenberg's signature. The cat owner picked up a pen and started to sign, but then stopped.

"Either you're the cheapest veterinarian in the world, or I got way more than a twenty percent discount."

Susan glanced at the slip of paper, which listed the total bill at twelve dollars. "I think a few numbers are missing."

Visibly flustered, Alice snatched the receipt. "I'm so sorry." Her face flamed and she spared another quick glance toward the man before ducking her head and turning again to the credit card reader.

Alice never made mistakes like that. Her fingers trembled as she punched the correct amount into the machine. The poor woman was obviously flustered, and the explanation sat in the Playful Pup room.

Compassion for her shy receptionist prompted Susan to offer an excuse. "We've been having trouble with that machine. We probably need to call the company and have them send a replacement."

Alice flashed her a grateful look.

When Mrs. Smellenberg had paid her bill, she reached for Taffy's carrier.

"Would you like some help out to your car?"

Susan asked.

"I'll help." Alice leaped up from her chair so quickly it rolled across the floor and crashed into the printer stand. At the same time, she knocked a stack of papers off the reception desk, and they fluttered to the floor. Thankfully, the man in the waiting room couldn't see behind the tall reception counter, but Alice, misery plain on her expression, probably didn't notice as she scrambled to retrieve them.

"Uh, that's okay." Mrs. Smellenberg shouldered her purse and, with a curious glance at Alice scooping papers off the floor, took Taffy's carrier from Susan.

When Susan had closed the door behind her, she turned toward the cause of Alice's agitation. "Hello. I'm Dr. Susan Hinkle."

He shook her hand. "Ansel Crowder." The name was spoken with the heavy Appalachian drawl common in eastern Kentucky.

"And who is this?" Susan stooped to rub the dog's ears. The breed had the reputation of being vicious, but most of the pit bulls she'd encountered were as friendly as any other. Like this one, who closed its eyes and leaned into her caress.

"This here's Goob." Ansel aimed an affectionate grin at his pet. "I aimed to call him

Butch, but when he was a pup he was such a bumbling little goober, he ended up being Goob." He leaned down and scrubbed the dog's neck roughly. "But you grew outta that, didn't ya boy?"

"Goob." Somehow she managed to keep a straight face while repeating the name. "Why are we seeing Goob today?"

"He went and got himself bit by something. Ain't sure what, but his hind leg's all swelled up and oozing."

A close inspection of the wound—two nasty-looking gouges—revealed the cause. "Looks like Goob surprised a snake. Maybe venomous from the looks of it, but definitely infected."

"I seen a cottonmouth by the crick a few weeks back." Concern settled over the man's broad face. "He'll be okay, won't he? I mean, he ain't gonna die from it?"

"I'm not at all concerned about that." Susan stood and gave him an assuring smile. "From the size of the fang marks, the snake was probably a baby and without enough venom to kill a big dog like Goob. I'm surprised he isn't sick, though."

"We-el, he has been kind of puny since yesterday. Sleeps a lot, and he's off his feed. He tends toward lazy, so I didn't think nothing of it until I saw him limping. The animal doc I go to over in Morleyville is on vacation, so I figured I'd give you a try." His gaze slid past Susan toward Alice. "Sure glad I did."

Though Susan managed not to look at her receptionist, she could almost feel the heat of another furious blush radiating from that direction. "I'm glad too. We'll get that cleaned up and give him some medicine that'll have him back to normal in no time. Let's take him to an examination room."

Passing the reception desk, she spared a quick glance at Alice, who was scribbling on a notepad, her head bent so far over her nose nearly touched the paper. Ansel stared hard at her as they passed, but she didn't look up. A grin threatened, which Susan suppressed. A little male admiration was good for any female's self-esteem, but especially Alice. As a single mother of five—including two rowdy boys who caused more trouble than a herd of coyotes—she often appeared exhausted and careworn.

"Yep." Ansel craned his neck to keep Alice in sight as he followed Susan through the swinging door to the clinic area. "Sure am glad I came to Goose Creek today."

Chapter Three

On Sunday night the phone rang just as Millie rinsed the last soapy dish and handed it to Albert for drying. She wiped her hands on a towel before picking up her cell. A glance at the screen revealed the caller to be her best friend.

"Hello, Violet."

"You need to get over here."

No preamble, no pleasantries. Not even an opening cliché, for which Violet was renowned. That in itself was enough to cause Millie concern.

"What's happened? Are you okay?"

"I'm fit as a fiddle. It's *them*."

The amount of disgust in the word left no doubt as to whom Violet was referring to. She had no fondness and little patience for the Thackers, who lived next door. Though she and Lulu had reached a kind of truce earlier that year, she found the couple unbearable and avoided them whenever possible.

"What have Lulu and Franklin done now?" Millie glanced at Albert, who turned from placing the clean skillet in the cabinet to give her his attention.

"I can't even begin to describe it. You'll have to see for yourself."

The call disconnected. Millie stared the phone for a few moments, her thoughts whirling. After Friday's conversation with Lulu, she suspected she knew the problem. Actually, she was kind of curious to see it herself.

"Get the car keys," she told Albert. "We've been summoned to Mulberry Avenue."

She expected a protest, because he had as little fondness for Franklin as Violet did. Instead, he went without a word to the hall closet and returned with their coats. Seeing them, Rufus leaped off of his bed and began to prance around Albert's feet, toenails tapping on the tiled floor.

Albert watched the beagle for a moment before saying, "Oh, all right. You can go too."

The air outside had turned frosty with the setting of the sun, and the drive to Mulberry Avenue wasn't long enough for the car's heater to warm up. Millie held her coat closed at the collar as her husband executed the turn onto the street where they'd lived for almost three decades.

"Good gravy, would you look at that?" Albert leaned forward over the steering wheel to peer through the windshield.

The Thackers' front yard glowed with a blinding rainbow of flashing lights. At first Millie couldn't make out any details, her eyes dazzled by the sheer volume of the garish display. As they approached the house, she was able to see better. Some of the ornaments merely glowed, like the small herd of reindeer in the center. Others blinked, while still others created the illusion of movement. A peacock appeared to spread his tail feathers, while nearby a glowing fountain sprouted glimmering blue streamers shaped to look like water. She caught sight of the frog just in time to see a string of pink lights zip from its mouth and snatch a bug from the air.

Albert pulled the car to the curb near a cluster of people on the sidewalk, gawking at the display. Violet detached herself from the group and joined Millie when she got out.

"Have you ever seen the like? It's tackier than a church bulletin board."

Millie shook her head, overcome by the sheer quantity of gaudiness. Albert rounded the car and joined them, Rufus trotting along beside him at the end of his leash. Rufus extended a nose toward their former yard, whimpered, and circled around to hide behind Albert's legs. The group of staring neighbors moved sideways to engulf them.

Don Rice shook his head slowly. "I never thought to see something like that in *your* yard, Al."

"It's not mine anymore." Only Millie knew the price Albert paid to reply in such a calm tone.

Carol, Don's wife, cast a longing glance at

Millie. "I wish you'd never moved. You were always so…" She appeared to grasp for a word. "So tasteful."

"Yeah," Violet agreed. "This looks like Munchkinland exploded, and we got hit by falling debris."

"Something has to be done." Doris Pulliam folded her arms across her chest. "Surely they're violating some sort of city ordinance."

"I've heard of codes against noise, but is there anything against lights?" asked Violet.

"We could call the mayor and ask," Carol suggested.

But Albert shook his head. "It's Thacker's property. He has the right to decorate it however he wants, just like any of us."

Millie gave her husband a shocked look. Never had she thought to hear him defending Franklin Thacker.

Doris shivered, whether from the cold or the view, Millie couldn't guess. "Maybe if we tell them how we feel, they'll listen."

"Good idea." Don turned on Albert. "You do it."

Albert took a backward step. "Me? No!"

"Don's right." Violet's lips tightened. "It's your fault they're here, so it's your responsibility to fix this."

Millie was about to leap to her husband's defense when the door to their former house opened, and the decorators themselves appeared. At least, she *assumed* it was the Thackers who emerged, though at first the glare prevented her from being certain.

Franklin's voice shouted a greeting. "Howdy, neighbors! We saw you out here admiring our decorations. They're something, aren't they?"

As he and Lulu threaded their way through the colorful Christmas mishmash, Violet muttered, "They sure are. Just what, I wouldn't dare to say."

Lulu approached Millie with a huge grin. "I told you they'd be awesome."

Millie found herself the subject of several heavy stares. Would her friends think her partially responsible for this vulgar spectacle? The smile she gave Lulu trembled. "I had no idea." She hoped that would appease their listeners. "It's far more colorful than you described, and more..." She grasped for a moment. "Well, just *more.*"

"I know they're amazing, but don't get used to them." Franklin wagged a finger at his neighbors. "They won't be here long."

Hope sprang into several faces.

41

"You're taking them down?" Carol asked.

"You betcha." Lulu turned and gazed with pride at her collection. "Soon as the town gets a gander at these, I'm gonna let the folks who own businesses take their pick. Just imagine how these'll look spread all up and down Main Street."

A long moment of silence followed as Millie, and presumably the others, did just that.

Franklin poked an elbow in Albert's ribs. "You can have your pick, buddy. A couple of these babies is just what you need in front of that big old house of yours."

Millie formed a silent prayer that Albert wouldn't embarrass her by saying anything insulting.

"Thanks for the offer." He pointed. "Those lighted deer over there would fit right in. And maybe that fountain could go in front of our gazebo."

Millie's jaw went slack. Surely Albert found the decorations as tawdry as everyone else. Why was he being so nice to the man he claimed regularly tap-danced on his last nerve?

Lulu planted her hands on her hips. "Now, Honey Bun, don't be too quick to give things away. I kind of had that fountain in mind for the front of Cardwell Drug Store. You know, 'cause it has a *soda fountain.*"

The two guffawed, Lulu even going so far as to bend over and slap her knee.

When her husband recovered, he grinned at her. "Whatever you say, Sugar Lips." Then he looked at his watch. "Oops! Gotta run, folks. My show's getting ready to start. But stay out here and look all you want. Like they say, looking's free."

Arm in arm, the Thackers wound their way between their blinking, twinkling, hodgepodge of holiday junk. When they disappeared inside the house, Millie turned to find everyone staring at her. Violet's expression in particular looked almost hostile.

She raised her hands in a posture of defense. "I knew she was going to buy a few decorations, but I had no idea it would be like this."

Amid mumbles they began to wander back to their homes.

Violet tugged her hat down over her ears. "At least I have thick curtains. Between now and New Year's, they're gonna be closed tighter than a clam at low tide."

As Al perused the online listings of job openings, his spirits sagged. Nothing new had been posted since yesterday. Every opening required experience in software he'd never used and some he'd never heard of. He picked up the cup resting on the table beside his laptop and drained it of its dregs. Before he had time to set the mug down, the waitress appeared.

"Another refill?" She held the coffeepot up.

"No, thank you. Six is my limit."

She glanced at the check, which she'd left three refills ago and he had not touched. "Okay. Let me know if you need anything else." Her smile appeared a tad forced.

She moved on to other customers, and Al glanced around the restaurant. No empty tables, and a couple of people standing near the door. Apparently he'd overstayed his welcome. He'd selected this small diner because it was off the beaten track, offered free Wi-Fi, and was located on the other side of town from his former place of employment. Who knew this little place would be so popular on a Tuesday morning?

He closed his laptop, slid it into his briefcase, and extracted his wallet. His fingers hovered for a moment over his credit card. No, Millie checked their financial activity online and would certainly question the expense. Instead, he extracted a few bills, hesitated, and then added several more. Best to leave a generous tip because he would probably be back.

He sat for a long time in his car, staring out the window. Where to next? There was a fast-food restaurant nearby that had complimentary Internet. But his watch showed that noon was not far off, and he didn't relish the chaos of the lunchtime rush. Neither did he look forward to a boring afternoon like yesterday, driving around town listening to talk radio, burning time and gasoline.

An idea struck, and he straightened in his seat. The library. Why hadn't he thought of that before? Not only did the library have computers, it had newspapers from all over. Tons of want ads to peruse. And librarians didn't care if people hung out there for hours.

His spirits brighter, he started the car.

Millie pulled the last bill off the printer and added it to the stack on the veterinary reception desk. "There you go. All ready to fold, stuff, and send out."

Alice, the afternoon receptionist, hovered nearby, waiting for Millie to vacate the only chair. "They'll go out in tomorrow's mail."

With a final glance at the desk's surface, Millie surrendered the chair to Alice. The action had taken on an official feel, like the changing of the guard at Buckingham Palace. In just over a year, when she and Albert retired, she would turn over the reception job to Alice completely. Already she'd backed off to only three days a week, ostensibly to allow her more time to work on readying the B&B for its eventual opening. In reality, she wanted to allow the single mother the opportunity to put in more hours. Alice needed the money worse than she did.

The muffled sound of a ringing phone came from the bottom drawer of the file cabinet. Millie hurried to retrieve her purse and fish out her cell. After a glance at the small screen, she could not hold back a moan. She'd been dreading this call since Sunday night. With a grimace, she pressed the button.

"Hello, Frieda. How are you today?"

"I'm shocked, that's what I am." The owner of the Freckled Frog Consignment Shop barked in a tone that made Millie wince. "How could you let this happen?"

No sense in pretending she didn't know what Frieda was talking about. "I haven't let anything happen. I tried to talk her out of buying all those decorations, but it's not my place to tell her how to spend her own money."

"I realize that, and if she wants to turn her yard into a National Lampoon look-alike, that's her business. But I'm telling you, not a single one of those atrocities will go on Main Street. I won't allow it."

Normally the comment would have irritated Millie. Frieda owned one of a dozen downtown businesses, and though she was certainly the most vocal, her role of spokesperson was self-appointed. Her opinion mattered no more than anyone else's.

Unfortunately, in this case the majority of the town would probably agree with her.

"I understand. And as long as every store up and down the street refuses, the matter will end there."

"But what if they don't? How do we know what Tuesday and Brett will do?"

Frieda had a point. The owner of Tuesday's Day Spa certainly did have eclectic tastes. She'd probably go into ecstasy over the peacock ornament. And it didn't take much imagination to picture Brett Hockensmith agreeing to a flashing, multicolored horse sculpture in front of his saddle and tack store.

Though Millie shuddered at the necessity, she offered a weak defense. "I don't see how we can stop them." She rushed on before Frieda could disagree. "Not that I want those gaudy things all over Goose Creek, but everyone has the same right as Lulu to decorate their property however they want."

Frieda answered in a tight voice. "What they do inside their stores is their own business. But we've got to stop them from putting cheap, trashy displays in their front windows, where they can be seen from the outside."

Susan emerged from the clinic area brushing black fur from her lab coat. Propping the phone against her ear with a shoulder, Millie took the lint roller from the file cabinet and handed it to her.

"I agree that we can say no to the light sculptures on public property, but when it comes to telling people how they can decorate their display windows, that's out of our hands."

Susan paused in the act of cleaning her right sleeve, her eyebrows arched. Millie rolled her eyes and mouthed, *Frieda Devall.* Susan gave a knowing nod.

"I refuse to let Goose Creek become a laughingstock. You need to put a rein on Lulu before she starts giving those things out, which I hear she's planning to do at the hanging of the greens on Friday." Frieda's voice became serious. "I'm sure the majority of the business owners will support me on this. Things could get ugly if we have to take sides."

Frieda's tone held a stubborn determination that Millie found a bit frightening. Once before Goose Creek's residents had been at odds over a public display—the painting of the town's iconic water tower. Though that had turned out well in the end, the battle had taken its toll in terms of damage to friendships. Christmas was not the time for another skirmish.

Resigned to her fate, Millie's shoulders sagged. "Fine. I'll talk to Lulu."

"Good. And do it today, before she does any more harm."

Though tempted to bristle at the commanding tone, Millie agreed and meekly ended the call. She dropped the phone in her purse and turned to find both Susan and Alice watching her.

"Trouble with the Christmas decorations, huh?" Susan gave her a sympathetic smile. "Justin and I drove over to see them last night.

49

They're kind of overwhelming."

"My kids love them." Alice shrugged. "They're only kids."

"Yes, well, Frieda is not a kid, and she definitely doesn't love them."

Susan finished with the lint roller and dropped it back into the drawer. "You look lovely today, Alice."

Millie shouldered her handbag and then took a closer look at Alice. She did look especially nice. Painfully shy, Alice usually dressed in shapeless clothing that gave her a rather mousy appearance. Today she wore a pretty print blouse and fitted slacks. And lipstick! Millie would have sworn Alice didn't own a lipstick. Maybe she borrowed her teenage daughter's. But why?

A blush stained her cheeks, and Alice muttered, "Thank you," while busying herself with straightening the stack of invoices.

Susan caught Millie's glance over Alice's head. "Who's on the schedule for the afternoon?"

"Oh, let's see." With movements that appeared carefully nonchalant, Alice tapped a key on the keyboard. "Mrs. Pennyweather is bringing her Siamese in for his annual shots, and Ben Hardister wants you to look at his Yorkie's ears.

Oh, and Ansel Crowder is bringing Goob back for a recheck of that snake bite."

At the mention of Ansel Crowder, the blush deepened, and Susan's grin became knowing. Aha! Did Alice have a beau?

Normally, Millie would have leaped on a matchmaking opportunity like this one. She had a soft spot for Alice and certainly wished her well, but today she had other things on her mind.

"I'll leave you to it, then. If you need help tomorrow, let me know. Otherwise, have a Happy Thanksgiving." She had taken Wednesday off to cook pies and other holiday goodies for their dinner up in Cincinnati with her sons' families.

"We'll be fine," Susan assured her. "Happy Thanksgiving to you, Millie. Have a safe trip."

Concern darkened Alice's pale eyes. "I hope you get everything worked out with those decorations so you can enjoy the holiday."

"That's my plan." Extracting her keys from her purse, Millie jingled them in a goodbye wave. "I'll go have a talk with Lulu right now before Frieda assembles a militia to take her down."

Chapter Four

T hat was a very nice Thanksgiving, don't you
think?"

Millie's question jerked Al back to the here
and now. With a start he realized they were only
a few miles from their exit. Instead of concen-
trating on steering the car down I-75, his mind

had been consumed with thoughts of his Shameful Secret, as he privately referred to it. Tomorrow would mark one full week since he'd been handed his walking papers, and he was no closer to a plan. At least the office was closed for the holiday weekend, so he wouldn't have to go to the pretense of dressing for work and finding something to occupy his time all day.

"Albert?"

He glanced at his wife, who wore an expectant expression. Oh. He hadn't replied to her question.

"Yes, it was. Crowded, though." Though there had been only three children present, in their son's small house they'd made enough noise for twice that many.

"I offered to have dinner at our house, but Rachel insisted on hosting since we're doing Christmas."

"She did a good job on the turkey." Because he knew his wife well, he was quick to add, "Not as good as you, of course. And the coconut cream pie was your best yet."

She awarded him a smile. "Everything was terrific. And Sarah and David's news made the day even more festive."

Their oldest son and his wife's announcement that they were expecting twins in the spring had come as a pleasant surprise. The couple's only child, six-year-old Abby, had walked around with her chest puffed out like the whole thing was her idea, which tickled Al. "They'll be like us, with one girl and twin boys."

"Except Abby will be an older sister, not the youngest like Alison."

A sigh followed the statement, heavy enough to cause Al to peer more closely at his wife. "I'd have thought you'd be jumping for joy at Sarah's invitation to come up and help with the babies when they arrive."

"Of course I'm happy." She didn't meet his gaze but toyed instead with a button on her coat. Was that a tear glittering in her eye?

"Out with it, Mildred Richardson. What's bothering you?"

Misery came to the fore, and a drop of salty moisture slid down the cheek closest to him. "It's at times like this when I miss Alison most. Imagine how Abby would have loved holding Melody, practicing to be a big sister."

Al said nothing. Every experienced husband knew there were times when silence was the wisest course of action.

After a moment, Millie continued, as he'd known she would. "Whenever we Skype, and I see my little girl holding *her* little girl and hear those baby coos through a cold computer speaker, I feel like my heart is being ripped out of my chest." A sniffle. "This Christmas is going to be the saddest ever."

Truer words were never spoken, but not, perhaps, for the reason Millie intended. Of course he missed Alison, but her move to Italy had been unavoidable. Her husband served as a junior officer in the military. Considering the state of the world, Italy was certainly better than most places he could have been stationed. Besides, infant Melody wouldn't know whether her grandparents were present or not, and by next Christmas they would be back in the States.

But this Christmas did promise to be the gloomiest of their thirty-eight-year marriage. How could Al pretend a festive mood when his career was over, his productive days at an end?

He thrust the thought from his mind. Plenty of time to dwell on that reality in the days to come. For now, his duty was to lift his wife's spirits. But how?

Inspiration struck. "I have an idea that's sure to cheer you up."

Hope flared in her eyes, and she twisted in the seat. "To fly Alison and the baby here for Christmas?"

Obviously she'd been harboring hopes that

weren't possible to fulfill. "That's not what I meant," he told her as gently as he could. "Even if we could afford the plane ticket, do you really think she would leave Nick alone for his daughter's first Christmas?"

More tears filled her eyes. "Couldn't he come too?"

"Millie, he's in the army. Getting that amount of leave over Christmas isn't easy. If he could, I'm sure they already would have arranged it."

She acknowledged the truth with a nod and plucked a tissue from the box on the console to blot the moisture from her eyes. "Then what is your idea?"

"Let's throw a Christmas party."

Ah, he'd surprised her. The tears evaporated, and she stared at him through ultra-wide eyes. Not that he blamed her. She knew his dislike of having outsiders invade his home, especially in quantities of more than two or three. But Millie adored entertaining, and the bigger the crowd, the better. If planning for a party would make her happy, he would suffer through a few hours' discomfort.

Besides, if she stayed busy planning a party, she would not have time to wonder at any odd behavior he might exhibit as he continued his search for another job. Or at least a plan of some kind, whatever that might turn out to be.

"We have the perfect party house. For Susan and Justin's wedding, you turned it into a real showplace. I'm sure when you finish decorating for Christmas, it'll be amazing."

Millie gave a slow nod, apparently warming to the idea. "Last year we didn't have nearly as many rooms finished as we do now. It would be nice to see them all dressed up for the holiday. We only had the one tree in the parlor last Christmas, but I've always envisioned a giant tree in the entry hall, and a small one in every guest room."

Under other circumstances, Al would have balked at the idea of more than a half-dozen Christmas trees. But if it brought the light back to his wife's eyes *and* gave him some breathing space to put together a plan for their future, he'd cut down an entire forest and haul it inside.

"I've always thought that big blue spruce in the front yard would look good covered in lights," he said.

She actually smiled. "And white lights on the shrubs by the porch railing." Then the smile turned upside down. "But no fake fountains or fly-munching frogs. And whatever possessed you to tell Franklin you wanted those lighted deer, anyway?"

The real truth—that he needed to stay on Thacker's good side—could not be uttered. Instead, he offered a lesser truth. "I thought they were the most tasteful of the bunch. I figured I'd better claim them then or we'd get stuck with the waving snowman."

"Good point." Millie faced forward and settled back in her seat, the sadness of a few moments before gone. "Actually, I don't think we have to worry about that anymore. When I talked to Lulu on Tuesday, she agreed to drop her idea of giving the decorations away to the Main Street business owners, but I had to push pretty hard. She finally admitted that Franklin enjoyed the attention their yard was getting, and they'd probably keep them all."

Al shook his head. "Do either of them have a clue how tacky people think those decorations are?"

"No, and I'm not going to tell them." She gave him a stern look. "And neither should you."

And risk alienating Thacker, who would blow the lid on his Shameful Secret?

"I won't," he promised.

The Friday after Thanksgiving turned out to be a perfect day for decorating Main Street. Though unseasonably cold, it seemed half the town showed up to help. Millie, bundled up in her warmest winter parka and fleece scarf, released the last of her sagging spirits as she helped her friends attach new scarlet bows to the silver and gold wreaths the town had used for about a decade.

She held up an artfully crafted bow and smiled at Frieda. "These are beautiful. I can't believe you did them all in a single day."

Frieda shrugged. "I couldn't make the trip to California to see my son, so it gave me something productive to do on Thanksgiving."

"You should have said something." Lulu, wearing a Santa hat and blinking elf-shaped earrings, sent Frieda a stern look over the top of the wreath she was working on. "I put on a real spread, and it was just Honey Bun and me. We're gonna be eating ham for months." She turned a buck-toothed grin on Violet. "Sorry you had plans yesterday, but we've got plenty of leftovers."

Violet kept her attention focused on her task

59

of wrapping wire around a wreath. "Thanks. I'll keep that in mind."

Lulu gave Violet's shoulder a playful, if overly aggressive, shove. "Girl, I'm gonna keep asking until you say yes." Then she picked up the wreath she'd been working on and headed down the street to turn it over to the hanging crew.

Violet grimaced after her. "She'll do it too. I'm in a pickle for sure."

Junior Watson had mounted a stepladder in the bed of his pickup and secured it with ropes. He drove it up and down Main Street, stopping at every light post to allow Little Norm Pilkington to hang a wreath. Norman, Little Norm's father, followed along on the sidewalk acting as supervisor, advisor, and cranky critic.

Norman pointed a gnarled finger and shouted up at his son. "'At un there's crooked. Turn it clockwise a smidge."

Millie glanced toward the south end of Main Street, where Albert worked with Franklin, Mayor Selbo, and a group of their fellow Creekers to wrap lights around a giant Douglas fir. The tree had been planted years before with Christmas in mind, and a grassy clearing surrounded it with iron benches, a perfect place to view Main Street in all its quaint, old-fashioned beauty.

Lulu returned with a new arrival in tow. "I brought us some help."

Tuesday Love, her mass of curls crowned by a hand-knit hat, picked up a bow. "This is real nice." She eyed Frieda. "Think you could do a couple purple ones for my front window?"

"Purple?" Frieda frowned. "I thought we were in agreement about the displays in the windows facing Main Street."

"Oh, we are." Tuesday nodded with vigor. "Only white lights. But for daytime, when the lights can't be seen, I went with a purple and silver garland and a nativity set that belonged to my grandma, the one who left me the money to buy my building." She grinned toward Millie. "It has a herd of sheep and angels and everything. That's okay, isn't it?"

Millie glanced at Frieda, who looked resigned. How could one argue with a nativity at Christmas?

"'Course it's okay." Lulu's brash voice left no room for argument. "It's your building." She, too, glanced at Frieda, whose bulging cheeks spoke of jaws clenched in an effort to hold her tongue.

"We'd best work faster." Millie ducked her forehead toward the stack of un-beribboned wreaths. "Otherwise we won't be done by sunset."

They picked up the pace and finished in time to help Lucy Cardwell ready the soda fountain in the drug store for the traditional gathering of decorators. By four thirty, huge urns of hot chocolate and coffee rested on the counter beside a stack of Styrofoam cups ready to be filled. Trays of cookies—donated by the female contingent of workers—filled the rest of the counter.

Millie eyed the offerings, a delectable variety of baked goods, and pondered the idea of making her Christmas party a potluck. A moment later she rejected the idea. The fun of having a party was preparing. She had selected the tenth of December as the date, which gave her only two weeks to bake all the goodies that would freeze well.

The decorating team filed in at a quarter to five, stamping frozen feet and reaching for hot beverages to warm their insides. Lucy turned on a CD of Christmas music, and the atmosphere inside the crowded drug store became festive.

At five thirty, Frieda banged a spoon on a metal cookie tray. "The sun has set, and it's getting crowded out there. I think it's time."

"Oh, goodie!" Tuesday clapped her hands like a delighted child. "This is so exciting."

Millie couldn't help but share her enthusiasm as she looped her arm through Albert's and followed the others outside.

Though remnants of sunlight still glowed in the western sky, darkness had triggered the lights on the wreaths. The sight of white lights nestled amid gold and silver lining each side of Main Street stirred excitement in Millie's chest. Most of the store owners had finished decorating their front windows as well, and the street was crowded with Goose Creek residents walking down the sidewalks on both sides of the railroad tracks, occasionally pausing to admire a display.

Millie and Albert made their way to the tree at the south end of town. They blended in with the throng of Creekers, ten deep in some places in a circle around the tree. Millie edged sideways so she could see around Little Norm, who was not little by anyone's standards. Up in the front, she spied the Wainright children, all five of them, with Alice standing guard behind them. She turned and spoke to the man beside her, who bent his head close to hear. Very close. Even from this distance, Millie clearly saw the shy smile Alice turned up to him, and Millie made a mental note to include *"Feel free to bring a guest"* on the party invitation she sent to Alice.

When the sidewalks were empty and everyone had found a place, Jerry and Cindie Selbo stepped into the center of the ring. He projected his voice loud enough to be heard.

"Welcome, everyone. This is one of my favorite duties as mayor of Goose Creek. I get to be the first to officially wish you Merry Christmas."

A dozen shouts returned the greeting. "Merry Christmas, Mayor!"

He waited until they fell silent. "Before we light the tree, I'd like to say thanks to the decorating team. Haven't they done a beautiful job?"

Applause, muffled by gloves and mittens, was overshadowed by an ear-splitting whistle. Millie was not surprised to identify the source as Lulu.

The mayor put on a broad grin. "Now let's welcome the Christmas season into our town."

After tonight, the tree would illuminate with a light sensor, like the wreaths, but for the official lighting ceremony, the mayor had the honor of performing the task by hand. Jerry bent over and pressed a connector. The Douglas fir erupted with color, a radiant display that dazzled Millie's eyes. From the lowest branches to the very top, every bow glowed with the flush of Christmas wonder.

A communal gasp rose from the gathering, followed by enthusiastic applause. Millie glanced over her shoulder, where Main Street stretched behind her, resplendent with old-town charm. The wreaths formed a glowing path that stretched from the far end of the street toward the beautiful evergreen. The white lights made the perfect complement to the stunning color of the tree.

Cindie stepped to her husband's side and began to sing. Soon everyone joined in a rousing rendition of "Jingle Bells." Though Millie had not been blessed with singing talent, she joined in with as much energy as anyone. When the song ended, an expectant hush fell over the assembled.

"This is my favorite part," Albert whispered, and she nodded.

Cindie began another song. Her beautiful voice rose clearly into the cold night sky. "Silent night, holy night."

Everyone joined in, and Millie's eyes were not the only ones that filled with tears as she sang from a full heart, "Sleep in heavenly peace."

On that joyful note, the crowd began to disperse. With a happy sigh, Millie hugged Albert's arm close as they headed for their car.

The Thackers fell in beside them.

Franklin grinned at Albert. "Merry Christmas, Bert!"

Millie felt her husband's muscles tense, but he answered in an easy tone that surprised her. "Merry Christmas, Franklin."

"Things sure are heating up at work, aren't they?" The man waggled his eyebrows.

Albert's arm tightened uncomfortably around hers. "Uh, yeah. Sure are."

A glance at his face revealed the oddest expression, one Millie recognized immediately as Albert hiding something. He had not mentioned a word about anything unusual at work. She opened her mouth to ask but then closed it when the reason occurred to her. He knew she was fretting over Alison's absence during the holidays, and he didn't want to worry her. What a sweet, considerate man she'd married.

Her guess was proven true when he immediately changed the subject. "Since you were on vacation this time last year, this was the first tree-lighting you've been to in Goose Creek. What did you think?"

"I gotta admit, that was a good time." Lulu shoved Millie's shoulder. "You were right about waiting for the day after Thanksgiving."

"And now that you see the wreaths in place,

don't you agree that sticking to them was the way to go?"

Lulu turned around and walked backward for a few steps, her gaze stretching down Main Street. "You know what I like most? The red bows. They break up all that boring white with a splash of color. We need something else." She faced forward again, frustration drawing deep lines on her forehead. "But since nobody wants light sculptures, I'm stumped."

Millie assumed a stern tone. "Everything is perfect, Lulu. Besides, it's too late to change now. The town is officially decorated."

"Baloney." Lulu blew a raspberry that produced a puff of mist in the cold air. "There's still thirty days till Christmas."

They reached the car, and Albert opened the door for Millie. The Thackers said goodbye and continued down the street in the direction of their house.

Settling herself in the seat, Millie watched the couple depart. An uneasy feeling niggled at her. Tomorrow she would call Lulu and rei-nforce the point that the time for decorating was over. If she had to threaten to involve Frieda, she would.

Chapter Five

The library was nearly deserted, a welcome change from last week when a whole herd of children on Thanksgiving break crowded the aisles and monopolized the computers.

Al closed his laptop, depression dragging his

mood to the vicinity of his shoes. The only responses he'd received to the dozen or so online applications he'd submitted were automatically generated e-mails saying, "Thank you for applying. Your application will be reviewed. If we are interested in scheduling an interview, we will contact you."

To make matters worse, his old job had been posted. Only it wasn't his job anymore. He didn't even meet the qualifications required to apply.

Relinquishing his claim to the table where he'd been stationed for the past three hours, he returned the stack of newspapers to the rack along the back wall. He'd scoured the want ads for papers from every city in Kentucky and Ohio. Cincinnati included a few possibilities, though not any that listed a salary even close to what he was accustomed to making. Still, if something came through there, he'd consider the ninety-minute commute each way. There was a slim possibility that the lure of living in the same town with three of their grandchildren—five when the twins arrived—would convince Millie to leave Goose Creek and the dream of her precious B&B. He didn't hold out much hope for that, though. Plus, they'd already sunk so much money into the house, he would probably have to work until he dropped dead at the office just to survive.

Briefcase in hand, he headed for the exit. He had to find a Kinko's or some other place to print the party invitations he and Millie had designed yesterday. His company—*former* company—allowed employees to use the office printers for a reasonable amount of personal printing, so Millie had assigned him the task. When he produced the printed invitations, he wouldn't say a word about where they'd been printed. That way he couldn't be accused of lying to his wife. Why, then, did guilt twinge at his conscience?

"Goodbye, Mr. Richardson." The librarian at the front desk paused in her task of removing books from the return bin. "Will we see you tomorrow?"

Al forced a smile. "Yes. See you then."
He left, wondering how long he would have to keep the Shameful Secret.

The veterinary clinic closed at three o'clock on Saturdays, three hours earlier than during the week. Susan had made the change after her wedding to give her and Justin more weekend time to spend together. She shut the door behind the last patient and turned toward the reception desk.

"I can hardly believe it's December third. Christmas will be here before we know it." She smiled at Alice. "Do you have plans for the weekend?"

The receptionist made a show of straightening the pens in the cup on the counter. "Well, yes. I mean, tonight I do."

A telltale flush colored her cheeks. In the past two weeks, Susan had noted that Alice's cheeks became rosy whenever a certain pit bull's owner was mentioned.

"Oh? A date, maybe?"

Her guess was confirmed when the blush deepened.

"Not really a date." Alice took a key ring from the desk drawer and busied herself locking the other drawers and the file cabinet. "Ansel offered to drive me to Lexington to do some shopping for the kids. And then we'll probably have dinner."

Susan couldn't stop a grin. How well she recognized those easy blushes and the way Alice avoided looking directly at her when questioned. It was just like when she first met Justin.

"Hmm. Dinner on a Saturday night sounds like a date to me."

To her surprise, Alice's head jerked up. Alarm drained the color from her face. "Do you think *he* thinks it's a date?"

Though curious, Susan felt a desire to put the anxious woman at ease. "Depends. I mean, if he asked you out to dinner, then it's a date."

"He didn't put it like that." She bit her lower lip, forehead creased. "He called yesterday and asked what I had planned for today, and I told him I needed to get over to Lexington and do some shopping. He said he had some to do too, so we should drive together to save gas, and then maybe we could grab something to eat on the way home." Her throat convulsed with a swallow. "Does that sound like a date?"

Of course it does. But at the dismay on Alice's face, Susan tempered her answer. "Maybe he's just being friendly."

Relief washed the lines from her brow. "That's what I thought too. Otherwise—" Her lips snapped shut.

How interesting. Susan had seen the two together at the tree lighting last week and had noted how attentive they were to each other. Because Ansel lived in Morleyville, he had no reason to attend the Goose Creek event unless he wanted to spend time with one of the residents. Namely, Alice. He'd done nothing to hide the fact. And Alice's attraction for the man couldn't be more obvious.

The question rested on the tip of Susan's tongue, but she bit it back. She considered both Millie and Alice friends, but they were also employees. Bosses shouldn't interfere in the personal lives of their staff unless invited to do so.

She kept her expression free of curiosity. "Have a good time. I hope you find some bargains."

Alice gathered her purse and rolled the chair neatly beneath the desk. "I'll see you Monday." Susan locked the door behind her. Why in the world did Alice want to avoid calling their outing a date?

Al stood on the sidewalk in front of his former home and watched as Forest and Heath Wainright handed the last reindeer to Junior, who put it in the bed of his pickup. Beside Al, Thacker rocked from heel to toe, hands shoved in his coat pockets.

"Are you sure you won't let me pay you?" Al made a show of reaching for his wallet, but Thacker held up a hand and shook his head.

"Not a penny. I'm glad to find a home for them. They take up a lot of space, and I've got a bid on eBay for a dancing Elvis that sings 'Blue Christmas.' Now I'll have room for him."

Al suppressed a shudder. The neighbors would be treated to sound in addition to light.

"Besides," Thacker continued in a stage whisper, "you need to save your money, being unemployed and all."

"Shhh." Al glanced around. "Keep your voice down."

"Relax, Bert. Nobody's listening. How long before you come clean, anyway?" He jerked his head toward the house. "I've never kept a secret from Sugar Lips this long. Not unless it was a surprise for her, and even then she always gets me to spill the beans."

"Not much longer. I have a lead on a couple of prospects." A bald-faced lie unless he wanted to move to Arkansas, where one company had a job opening for which he might be qualified. He'd applied while at the library yesterday, but if he landed the job, he knew full well he wouldn't be able to take it. No way would Millie go to Arkansas. Still, an offer would prove that he wasn't useless, that *somebody* still wanted him.

Junior slammed the gate of the pickup. "I'll see ya over at your house." With a wave in Al's direction, he climbed into the cab and started the truck.

The boys ran to join Al and Thacker.

Forest skidded to a halt. "Those are gonna look real good in your front yard, Mr. Richardson." He blew a bubble and sucked it back in.

"I think Mrs. Richardson wants to put them in the back near the pond," Al told the boy. "That way people can see them from the verandah."

Heath bounced up and down. "Can you turn on the frog, Mr. Thacker? I love watching him eat that bug."

Thacker laughed but shook his head. "Wouldn't be able to see much in the daylight, would we? Come back later, and I'll turn them all on."

"We've been here 'bout every night," Forest said. "Your yard is the awesomest in the whole town."

Thacker gazed around his lawn, his shoulders back and chest puffed out. "It is, isn't it?"

If you're ten years old. Al kept the comment to himself and, thanking Thacker again, herded the boys into the car.

When they turned off of Mulberry Avenue, Heath spoke from the backseat. "Mr. Richardson, Mama said everybody in town is upset at Mr. Thacker on account of those lights. How's come?"

How does one explain tastelessness to a pre-adolescent boy who no doubt prized quantity over quality?

Al chose his words carefully. "I wouldn't say *everybody* is upset. But some people think that's too many decorations for one yard."

"Then why don't they ask him if they can have some for their own yards, like you did?" The boy's tone became sulky. "We asked Mama if we could get some, but she said no on account of we're renting and the landlord might not allow it."

Because Al knew the Wainrights' landlord to be an easygoing man, he surmised Alice herself wasn't interested in decorating with light sculptures. He adjusted the rearview mirror so he could see the backseat. "It could be that they don't like those particular decorations."

"I don't see why anybody wouldn't want that frog." Heath unwrapped a fresh piece of bubblegum, popped it in his mouth, and pocketed the wrapper.

"Or that camel with the neck that moves up and down," Forest added. "I wish you'd gotten that one for your yard."

For a moment Al envisioned Millie's reaction if he arrived at home with the camel and its companion piece, the donkey. Even at his bravest, he would not willingly fight that particular battle.

"I think Mrs. Richardson has different ideas for decorating our yard."

A glance in the mirror revealed two perplexed expressions. In the past five months, since the fiasco that these two miscreants had masterminded at Justin and Susan's wedding, they'd displayed a sincere desire to make amends. Al wasn't the only one who had been impressed with the energy with which the two had tackled the clean-up project they'd been assigned as punishment for their misdeeds. So yesterday, when Alice called with her babysitting request, Millie had jumped at the chance to have the Wainright children over for an afternoon and evening and had immediately begun planning activities for them. Even now, Fern and Willow and little Tansy were in Millie's kitchen, learning to bake delectable treats. Millie had also informed Al that she intended to pay them for their help. He might have balked had he not developed a soft spot—a small spot, only about the size of a dime, of course—for the fatherless urchins.

Though likely to confuse them, maybe the kids deserved an honest answer. "It's like this, boys. Most people in town think those light sculptures are ugly." He hurried to forestall any differing opinions. "I know you don't agree, but everybody is entitled to his own opinion. And in most cases, a few decorations are plenty, but when the yard is so full you can't even walk in it, people think it's overdone."

"They think too many lights are gross?" Forest asked.

"Gross." Al nodded. "Exactly."

"Well, I don't." Heath folded his arms across his skinny chest. "I like 'em."

Actually, Al harbored an unvoiced fondness for the motorcycle piece that he dared not share with anyone over the age of twelve. Especially his wife. "Me too," he told them. "Some of them."

They arrived home then, and Al pulled onto

his long driveway to find Junior already unloading the reindeer.

He glanced again in the rearview. "You boys ready to work? I want to get those deer in place now so you'll be able to help me hang garland on the front porch before supper."

"You bet, Mr. Richardson," Forest said.

"Let's get 'er done!" chimed in Heath.

Chapter Six

Alice arrived at work Monday afternoon with a despondent frown, her shoulders slumped, and dark, sagging pouches beneath her eyes. Susan exchanged a concerned glance with Millie.

"Are you feeling okay?" Susan asked as the

woman dropped her purse into a filing cabinet drawer.

Alice gave a distracted nod. "I didn't sleep well last night, but I'm fine."

Millie peered into her face. "Maybe you're coming down with something. If you want to take the afternoon off, I'll cover for you."

"It's quieter here." A brief, rueful smile flashed onto her pale lips and disappeared as quickly. "All the kids are stuck in the house because of the rain."

With the unseasonably cold December this year, rain could turn to sleet without warning. Definitely not amenable for active children like the Wainright boys.

"Well, if you're sure." Millie slipped on her coat and took her umbrella from the stand by the door. "Call me if you change your mind."

When they were alone, Susan started to head back to Exam Room One, where a kitty with a digestive disorder waited, but then she hesitated. The difference in Alice from Saturday's pleasure in her not-a-date plans with Ansel Crowder was marked. With their full afternoon schedule, this might be the only chance they'd have to talk in private.

"Are you sure there's nothing wrong? Because you look unhappy about something." She paused delicately: "How did your outing with Ansel turn out?"

Bingo. Tears filled Alice's eyes. "It was wonderful. We had a great time."

"Then why are you upset?"

The receptionist snatched two tissues from the box on the counter. "Because when we finished shopping, he took me to a steak restaurant and insisted on buying my dinner."

No doubt about the meaning of that gesture. "So it really was a date."

Alice nodded.

"Did you have a good time?"

Another nod, and she blew her nose.

"Help me understand something here." Susan perched on the edge of the desk. "A nice man who is clearly attracted to you asks you out, helps you shop for your kids, and then buys your dinner. I don't see the problem."

No answer came at first. Alice wadded the tissues into a ball, tossed them into the trash can, and plucked another from the box. Her throat convulsed repeatedly. Susan waited, giving her time to regain her composure.

Finally, she drew in a deep breath and blew it out. "The problem is that I'm married."

Surprised, Susan couldn't come up with a response. Married? Though she had never asked, she'd assumed Alice was divorced. Or maybe widowed, because she had never heard any mention of the kids' father coming for a visit.

Alice spread the tissue out on the desk and folded it into a neat square as she explained. "He's an addict. He always drank, but then he hurt his back falling off a ladder, and they gave him pain pills. That was when Heath was a baby. When his prescription ran out and the doctor wouldn't give him anymore, he went to another doctor, and another. Then he started buying them on the street. Things went downhill fast. Cocaine. Heroin. He couldn't hold a job. I was working in a restaurant in Louisville, trying to pay the bills, but he always found the hiding place for my tip money and bought drugs."

The words were flowing faster now. Alice obviously wanted to confide in someone.

Susan asked, "He wasn't willing to go to rehab?"

A bitter laugh passed Alice's lips. "Oh, sure. He went three times. Once on his own, and twice more because he was court-ordered. Willow was born while he was in rehab the second time. He'd get clean for a while, but it never lasted. The last straw came when I was pregnant with Tansy." She kept her gaze fixed on her fingers, which folded the tissue over and over again. "I opened the trunk of the car and found a backpack with a bunch of stuff in it. Drain cleaner. Antihistamine tablets. Lithium batteries and something called liquid fire. And a big plastic bottle with white stuff in the bottom."

That combination of ingredients could only be used for one thing. Susan recognized them from television news reports. "He was making methamphetamine."

Alice nodded. "In the same car we used to drive the kids around. We fought, and I ended up with a broken jaw."

Knots pulled tight in Susan's stomach, and with an effort she unclenched her fists. "So you turned him in?"

To Susan's surprise, Alice shook her head. "I wanted to. I should have. But I couldn't do it. Instead I gave him an ultimatum—either give up the drugs for good or leave. He left. We haven't heard from him since." The tears returned, and she shook out the folded square of tissue to wipe her eyes. "The whole time I was carrying Tansy, I was terrified she'd have something wrong with her because he was using when I got pregnant. Thank the Lord she was perfect."

Susan had attended Tansy's fourth birthday

party a few months ago. That meant Alice's husband had been gone for close to five years. "Have you ever tried to contact him?"

"I've thought about it a lot, but I wouldn't know where to start. And when Fern got into trouble, I knew I couldn't subject the kids to an addicted father who obviously didn't care enough to contact them."

Alice's oldest daughter had worked for Cardwell Drug Store and was caught stealing antihistamines and other meth-making materials. When Susan moved to Goose Creek, Fern was confined in a juvenile detention center. How awful that must have been for Alice, to see her oldest daughter following in the steps of her addict father. Thank goodness Fern was doing well now.

Through the window Susan glimpsed a car pulling into the small parking lot. They were about to be interrupted.

"Listen, if you do want to find him, maybe I can help. One of Justin's motorcycle buddies is a state police detective. He'll be discreet. And if he finds out your husband is still in bad shape or even in jail, at least you'll know."

A fearful expression overtook her features, but then she bit down on her lower lip and gave a slow nod. "Maybe it's time."

Outside, an umbrella popped open above the driver's side door, and a woman emerged holding a pet carrier. Susan examined Alice's blotchy face, which showed evidence of crying and would definitely become fodder for the gossip chain.

"You go freshen up. I'll check Mrs. Barnes in." Susan tapped on a notepad. "Before you leave this evening, write down any information you can about your husband, and I'll give it to Justin's friend."

With a grateful nod, Alice retrieved her purse and headed for the bathroom.

Millie's cell phone interrupted her work on the veterinary clinic's Wednesday bank deposit. She glanced at the screen and heaved a sigh. Calls from Lulu never ended quickly.

"Hello, Lulu."

"The peacock's gone!"

Millie jerked the phone away from her ear, and the shriek through the speaker was clearly heard by those seated in the Kuddly Kitty waiting room. Curious stares fixed on her. She swiveled the reception chair around to face the back wall.

"Another light sculpture is missing?" This was the third in as many days. One a night since Sunday.

"Stolen. And that was my favorite too." Outrage gave Lulu's voice a high-pitched whine that shot through the phone and grated across Millie's nerves. "We're the victims of burglary. Frankie thinks we should report it to the police."

"I can't imagine who would take those"— Millie bit off the words *hideous things* in the nick of time—"decorations. Especially since you offered to give them away."

"Whoever took them are not putting them up. Frankie and I drove all over Goose Creek and Morleyville after supper last night. No sign of the snowman or the fountain."

"And you didn't see anything during the night?" After Monday's theft, the Thackers had planned an all-night vigil to watch for the thief 's return.

"We fell asleep. Woke up around two and took inventory. Nothing missing, so we figured the crook had stolen what he wanted and we went to bed. Got up this morning to find my peacock missing."

Aware of the attentive silence in the waiting room behind her, Millie lowered her voice. "Maybe you *should* call the police. Those things aren't cheap, after all, even if you did get a bargain."

"I'm afraid to, and that's the plain truth." Lulu's tone lost some of its edge. "Frankie thinks somebody's stealing them because they want them, but I'm not so sure."

"What other reason would the thief have?"

"C'mon, girl. You know as well as I do that some folks aren't as fond of them as you and me."

Pinpricks of shame stabbed at her. She hadn't actually claimed to *like* the decorations, but to spare Lulu's feelings she had uttered a few words of admiration for one or two of them. Things like, "If you narrow your eyelids, that fountain looks like it really could be spraying water," and "Isn't it amazing how the lights are perfectly synchronized to make it look like the candle flame is actually flickering?"

For the benefit of her audience, Millie made a pretense of opening a drawer and flipping through the files inside. She lowered her voice even more. "Why would someone steal something they don't like?"

"So they don't have to see it anymore. It might be someone on Mulberry Avenue." Her voice took on an ominous tone. "Maybe even right next door."

Millie immediately leaped to her friend's defense. "That's ridiculous. Violet would never do anything so spiteful."

Privately, though, she wondered. Violet certainly did detest the ostentatious display, and had complained about it at some length the last time they talked.

"What about Frieda? She's had a burr under her saddle ever since we put them up."

"Only because she didn't want them downtown. I'm sure she doesn't care what you do with your own yard."

"That's another thing. I'm working on another idea about Main Street, one she can't argue with. But anyway, I'd hate to set the cops on somebody we know. That'd make things awkward around here."

Even the accusation would alienate the Thackers from their neighbors. They didn't have many friends to begin with.

"That's a good point. Maybe you should try to stay up again tonight and see if you can catch whoever-it-is in the act."

"That's what I think too." Lulu sounded relieved. "I'll tell Honey Bun that's the plan."

When they disconnected the call, Millie immediately dialed another number.

"H'lo?"

Millie straightened, alert to Violet's tone. Definitely not her usual cheerful answer. "Are you sick?"

"'Course not. You caught me napping." The sentence ended with a yawn.

Suspicion stabbed at Millie. "In the middle of the morning?"

"I'm so tired today I'm not worth a plugged nickel. As lazy as a fat cat on a hot summer day." Another yawn. "So what's up?"

"Another of Lulu's light sculptures is missing."

The news perked Violet right up. "Really? Was it the frog?" A note of hope rang in the question.

The ladies in the waiting room had gone utterly still, and a glance confirmed that Millie commanded their full attention. She rose and stepped through the swinging doors into the clinic area.

"No, the peacock." Was there a delicate way to phrase the question that must be asked? "You wouldn't know anything about these nightly thefts, would you?"

"Only that I wish the culprit would take the really ugly ones instead of the smallest." A sucked-in breath sounded through the phone. "Wait a minute. Are you accusing *me*?"

The offense in her tone could not be faked. Millie rushed to cover her tracks. "Of course not." *Think quick, Millie.* "Since you live next door, I thought you might have heard something in the night." Inspiration struck. "Maybe that's what interrupted your sleep."

"Oh."

The explanation appeared to have placated Violet, and Millie sank against the lab counter. They'd been friends for decades, and though Violet did not take offense easily, she could be prickly where the Thackers were concerned.

"Truth be told, I couldn't sleep on account of eating chili for supper. I musta put in too much cayenne, 'cause it was hotter than Peter Piper's peppers. I hate to throw out the leftovers, but I can't handle another night like that."

"Add sour cream," Millie advised. "That'll cut the heat and make it tasty besides."

"Good idea. Anyway, I didn't hear a peep from next door. But if I had, I wouldn't tell *them*. Why look a gift horse in the mouth? If I'm lucky, the thief will keep coming back."

Her fears about Violet allayed, Millie ended the conversation and returned to her desk. Of course, Violet wasn't the only resident of Mulberry Avenue who disliked the ostentatious display. What if the culprit was another neighbor?

Maybe one more phone call was in order. Though she tried not to bother Albert at work unnecessarily, maybe he could talk to Franklin and make him see the sense in leaving the police out of the picture. For now anyway.

"Gooooooood morning. Franklin Thacker here."

Speaking of Franklin. "Hello. This is Millie."

"Oh! Uh...hey, Millsie. How's it shaking down your way?"

Millie winced. Franklin loved to come up with nicknames for those he liked. A form of affection, no doubt, but Millie disliked being called *Millsie* nearly as much as Albert hated *Bert.*

"Since you're answering Albert's phone, I assume he's away from his desk."

"You could say that. Yeah. He's definitely not in his cubicle."

Something sounded odd about Franklin's voice. "Do you know where he is?"

"Nnnnnnnooooo, can't say I do."

Odd. One of the things Albert complained

about was the way Franklin kept tabs on his whereabouts, even timing his visits to the men's room.

"When he comes back would you ask him to call me?"

"Uh, yes. I can give him a message."

Franklin didn't sound like his usual jovial self. Millie couldn't put her finger on it. Not distracted, exactly. More like…cautious.

Maybe he'd been in the middle of a project. Albert disliked being interrupted when he was working on a program, and sometimes his replies were gruff enough to hurt her feelings.

"Thank you. I'm sorry to interrupt you at work."

"No problemo, Millsie. Have a good day."

She replaced the receiver and stared at it for a long moment. A strange man. He and Lulu were perfectly matched.

A comment from her conversation with Lulu returned, one she'd let pass at the time. What new idea about decorating Main Street did the woman have? Dread gathered in the pit of Millie's stomach. Surely she wouldn't attempt anything else with Christmas only two and a half weeks away. Maybe she was referring to an idea for next year's decorations. Yes, that must be it. Putting the Thackers out of her mind, Millie swiveled around and returned to work.

Al's cell phone rang, drawing a disapproving stare from the nearest librarian. He snatched it up and flipped it open.

"Richardson here."

"Man, I just about blew your cover!"

Thacker.

Al pressed the phone closer to his ear. "What do you mean?"

"Millsie called. She wanted to know where you were."

Alarm bells clanged in Al's mind. "What did you tell her?"

"The truth. That I didn't know where you were, but I'd give you a message. I had sweat dripping down my back."

Al wilted in his chair. "Thanks, Franklin."

"Listen, buddy, I don't know how much longer I can keep this up. I gave up lying years ago on account of I'm no good at it. Sooner or later Lulu's going to figure out I'm keeping a secret and ask me outright what it is. The only reason she hasn't so far is because she's obsessed with this decoration thing."

"It won't be much longer. I'm close to a plan." Al glanced at the laptop screen, which showed he'd reached level six on Candy Crush.

"Good." Curiosity colored Thacker's voice. "What do you do all day, anyway?"

"I'm looking for a job and…" The colorful game board winked on his screen. "…developing new skills."

"I can't figure you out, Bert. If somebody gave me a chunk of change to retire early, I'd do backflips all the way home."

"You'll feel differently if it happens to you." He clicked on the reshuffle button and watched the game board reconfigure itself. "I'd better call Millie. Thanks again."

He took a moment to settle his nerves before dialing his wife's number. He didn't like deceiving Millie any more than Thacker. Was it time to admit defeat and come clean? It had been two and a half weeks since he lost his job, and he was no closer to landing another one than that fateful day. Even the Arkansas corporation had rejected him.

But he had a few more applications about which he hadn't heard. One was to a recruiting firm that boasted they found employment for 95 percent of their clients. Those places had connections and knew about jobs that the public didn't.

Today was Wednesday. Millie's Christmas party was only three days away, on Saturday evening. Only a heel would deliver a blow like this right before an event that his wife had been frantically planning for weeks. She didn't need anything else to distract her, nothing to stress her out. Besides, maybe he'd hear something within the next few days.

He'd give it until this weekend, and if nothing had turned up by Sunday, he'd sit Millie down and break the news.

For now, he needed to come up with a plausible reason for calling her from his cell instead of the office phone. Not a lie. Like Thacker, Al couldn't lie to his wife. Not only would she spot it in an instant, the guilt would eat him alive. So he'd tell the truth. That he was at the library doing research. That would be unusual enough she might question him about the project, but he would find a reason not to explain at the moment. If Lulu was distracted with decorations, Millie was distracted with the Christmas party. It would work, and he wouldn't utter an untrue word.

So why did he feel as if he might throw up?

"How are you feeling, fella?" Susan squatted in front of the kennel to rub the ears of the lab mix from which she'd just removed a fatty tumor. Benign, as she'd known it would be. "Your owner will be here after work to pick you up."

The dog made a feeble attempt to wag his tail, but his eyes refused to stay open. Still groggy from the surgery.

"That's okay. Just sleep. You'll feel better soon."

Reassured that the dog was recovering, she closed the kennel and then washed her hands at the sink. The door separating the clinic area from the waiting room swung inward, and the last person she expected to see entered.

"Justin!" Her heart fluttered in her chest, as it always did when she saw her handsome husband of five months. She crossed the room and flung herself into his arms, breathing deeply of the pleasing blend of his aftershave and the musky aroma of his skin. "What a nice surprise. But I thought you were painting a house in Frankfort today."

"I was until Jeff called. He asked me to ride over here with him."

Jeff Howard, the state police detective Justin had asked to look into the whereabouts of Alice's husband.

Susan pulled back and gazed into Justin's face. "Is the news bad?"

He nodded. "He's telling her now. She might need some support."

With an arm around her waist, he pulled her into the reception area. Because Friday mornings were reserved for surgeries, the waiting rooms were empty. Alice perched on the edge of a white plastic chair, her gaze fixed on the detective's face. He held a thin folder in his hands. His thumb constantly rubbed one edge. A nervous gesture, perhaps? He glanced up, acknowledged their arrival, and then continued speaking.

"From there it looks like he drifted west and ended up in Texas. I talked to a border patrol agent who said they'd had him under surveillance for suspicion of trafficking."

"Drugs?" Alice asked, her voice small.

The detective nodded. "Cocaine and heroin. They got wind of a deal going down involving one of the Mexican drug cartels and were putting plans in place for a raid. Said the mood was tense, and their informant disappeared. Next thing they knew, they got a call about some bodies out in the brush just this side of the border. Multiple gunshot wounds from an AK47, the preferred weapon of a prominent cartel down there. One of the deceased was their informant." He paused, and compassion stole across his features. "The other was your husband."

Alice's face crumpled, and she covered it with her hands. Susan crossed the room and sat beside her, lending support with an arm around her shoulders.

"Are...are they sure?" Alice finally asked. "That it was Stuart, I mean."

"Yes, ma'am. They had his fingerprints on file from prior arrests."

Justin asked the question in Susan's mind. "Why didn't they contact Alice?"

"They didn't know he was married. The officer I spoke with said they found his arrest records from Kentucky and notified Jefferson County, but the people who lived at the last address on file had never heard of him."

"It was an apartment," Alice whispered. "I left a forwarding address when we moved here, but that was several years ago."

"In cases like this, it's not unusual to let the matter drop. Police departments everywhere have more work than they can handle, so if nobody comes looking..." Jeff shrugged.

Only Alice's soft sobs broke the silence that followed. Susan squeezed her shoulders.

"If he was killed with an informant, is it possible he might have been helping the police to catch the drug dealers?"

At Justin's question, Alice uncovered her eyes, her expression hopeful.

Jeff looked doubtful, but before he could speak Susan gave him a hard look. The least he could do was offer a shred of hope, even if it was false.

He took the hint. "Anything's possible."

Susan firmed up her hug. "Maybe that's what you could tell the children. It might make the news easier for them to hear."

But Alice shook her head. "No. Fern remembers enough to figure out the truth, and the others don't need to hear details. I'll tell them their daddy moved to Texas and died there. That's enough." She straightened and lifted her head high. "But I'm not going to tell them anything just yet. Stuart spoiled too many Christmases when he was with us. There's no reason to let him spoil this one too."

Despite the show of bravado, Susan spied a fresh welling of tears when Jeff handed her the folder containing the details he'd uncovered.

"Why don't you take the rest of the day off ?" She almost said she could call Millie to fill in, but then remembered Millie was drowning under a ton of arrangements for her Christmas party tomorrow. "The afternoon schedule's pretty light. I can handle it by myself."

Alice managed a grateful smile but again shook her head. "I'll be fine. Really. And besides, I need the hours." She stood and, holding the folder in her left hand, offered her right to Jeff. "Thank you for finding out. I appreciate it."

"You're welcome. I'm sorry for your loss."

To which Alice shook her head sadly. "We lost Stuart a long time before he disappeared."

Though Alice's sobs had stopped, the truth behind that statement brought tears to Susan's eyes.

Chapter Seven

The pungent odor of silver polish overrode the delectable aroma of baking chicken. Seated at the kitchen table, Al rubbed the last bit of tarnish from a spoon and set it with the others. Polishing silver had to be his least favorite chore in the world, but today he tackled the project with enthusiasm. Anything was better than hanging out at the library playing mindless video games.

Actually, the entire day had been far more pleasant than expected. Working alongside Millie to get things ready for the party reminded him of their early days, before the kids came along, when he'd rush home from the office eager to spend his evening hours helping her cook supper, or hang pictures, or pull weeds in the garden. Whatever task she had to do, he'd been glad to work at her side because simply being with Millie made even the dullest chore joyful.

"I'm almost finished. What's next on my list?"

She spoke without turning from the kitchen counter where she applied a chopping knife to a pile of onions with relentless energy. "Fetch the coffee urns from the attic and wash the dust out of them."

"Yes, ma'am, Sergeant Richardson." He gave a mock-salute with the last unpolished spoon.

Turning, she awarded him a sheepish smile. "I'm sorry. I don't mean to bark orders."

He grinned to show he took no offense. "I'm your slave for the day, so order away."

Abandoning the onions, she crossed the

Virginia Smith

room and wrapped her arms around him from behind. "Do you know how much I appreciate you?"

"Because of my superior silver-polishing skills?" He held up the gleaming flatware.

"That too." She kissed the top of his head. "But mostly because you took a vacation day to help me get ready for the party. I know you're super busy with that special project at work."

Guilt stabbed at him. "It's not a big deal. They don't really need me."

Truer words had never left his lips.

"Of course they do. That place would collapse without you." One more kiss and she returned to her work. "But today I need you more, and I'm grateful you volunteered without my having to ask."

His good mood gone, Al finished his task in silence. When every piece of silver had been returned to the velvet-lined case, he headed for the attic.

Millie's shout followed him down the hall. "The urns are in the box marked Kitchen #3."

He trudged up the attic stairs, his footsteps heavy. What a jerk he'd become. Worse than Thacker, who was the biggest nitwit he knew. Millie's gratitude was too much to bear. From the beginning of their marriage, he'd been keenly aware he didn't deserve such a wonderful woman, and his deception of the past few weeks merely proved him right. What was the matter with him? Why had he allowed this to continue?

The answer was painful to admit. Pride. He'd been so concerned about being considered weak, about handing over the role of breadwinner to his wife, that he'd allowed himself to become a loathsome creep. How he longed to come clean, to sit her down, and unburden the Shameful Secret that burned in his chest.

Sunday couldn't come fast enough.

He returned with the coffee urns to find her tapping on her tablet. Worry lines creased her brow.

"The weather forecast looks terrible. They're predicting a winter storm tomorrow night."

He'd been tracking that storm for several days. "Look on the bright side. We might have a white Christmas."

"Christmas is fine, but I don't want the weather to interfere with the party. What if nobody comes?" She waved a hand toward the mountain of chopped vegetables. "We'll be stuck with enough chicken salad to feed half the state."

"People will come," he assured her. "Probably more than the house can hold. And judging by the amount of cooking you've done in the past couple of weeks, we'll *still* be stuck with more leftovers than we can handle."

She set the tablet on the table and turned toward the sink. "Oh, Albert, look. The wind has blown over one of the reindeer."

"We haven't had any wind strong enough to do that."

"Well, something knocked it over. Look."

Sure enough, one of the four lighted reindeer he'd set up near the pond lay on its side.

"I'll take care of it."

Shrugging on his coat, he exited the house. Rufus dashed outside on his heels and then darted past him, barking. The dog had been fascinated with the deer since they'd arrived. Not the brightest of animals, he acted as if he thought they were live invaders of his territory.

"They're not real," Al shouted after him. "Don't be a dunce."

As Al trudged across the yard, Rufus took up a stance in front of one of the statues, barking like a crazed hound. He leaped forward, snapped at a wire leg, and then hopped backward to bark some more. The third time he snagged the wire in his teeth and jerked. The deer teetered.

"Mystery solved." Al grabbed the dog by the collar and hauled him back. "Leave it!"

To his surprise, Rufus obeyed. After another few barks, he trotted off in the direction of the pond. Shaking his head, Al righted the overturned statue. He turned toward the house only to be stopped when Rufus began another barking fit.

"Now what?"

Something on the opposite side of the pond had captured the dog's attention. He stared at the ground, unmoving, and filled the air with excited barks. Curious, Al headed in that direction. Probably a leaf or a bug or something equally threatening.

As he neared, the shimmer of blue tinsel in the grass caught his eye.

"What in the world?"

Then he recognized the item. He hurried forward, bent down and grasped the wire edge of Thacker's fountain-shaped light sculpture.

Rufus stopped barking and bounded away. Al looked after him and saw Millie approaching, buttoning her coat.

"I came to see what all the fuss was about." Eyes wide, she pointed at the decoration. "How did that get here?"

"I have no idea." Straightening, Al scanned the area and immediately located the other two missing sculptures.

"There's Lulu's peacock." Millie paced across the winter-brown grass and lifted the light-covered wire. "It doesn't look damaged."

"There's the snowman." Al pointed toward the third, and then scanned the area. To one side of their property lay a cattle field. A horse farm wrapped around the other side and the back, hidden behind a thick stand of evergreens that afforded them year-long privacy. Both were protected by fences, and though the decorations weren't heavy, they would be awkward to lift over a fence. The only other way to get back here was through the yard, past his house.

He pointed at their driveway, where his motor home was parked. "I'm guessing whoever stole these came right down our driveway and skirted around the RV."

"But why bring them here?" Millie shook her head. "Is somebody trying to make it look like we took them?"

Discomfort squeezed Al's insides. Was this an attempt to stir up trouble between him and Thacker? And if so, why? Of all times to cause problems with the guardian of his Shameful Secret, this was the absolute worst.

Something on the ground caught his eye. A small white scrap caught in the tinsel-wrapped wire. Stooping down, he plucked the paper from the decoration.

Holding it between his fingers, he awarded Millie a triumphant look. "I know who did it."

When Thacker arrived home from work, Al was waiting for him. Beside him on sidewalk stood the Christmas decoration thieves, their tousled heads bowed with shame. Forest looked like he might be sick, and Heath sniffled in an obvious attempt to hold back tears. Lulu hovered over them like a mother hen.

Thacker emerged from his car. "What's up, Bert? Come to gawk with the kiddos?"

"Not exactly." Al placed a hand on each child's back and gave a gentle shove. "The boys have something to tell you."

Forest's head dropped even further, and he mumbled something unintelligible.

"What's that?" Thacker bent toward him. "You want to look at the lights?"

"Not *look*." Heath drew in a breath. "Took.

We took 'em."

Surprise erupted on Thacker's face. "You? You're the thieves?"

Lulu stepped between him and the boys. "Now, Honey Bun, don't be upset with them. Wait till you hear why."

"We were trying to help." Forest looked up, his expression earnest. "So people wouldn't be mad at you anymore."

Heath agreed with an energetic nod.

Thacker looked from one to the other, scratching his head. "What makes you think people are mad at me?"

"'Cause Mr. Richardson said so."

"Whoa, hold it right there." Al lifted his hands. "All I said was some people might think there were too many lights for one yard." Thacker's eyebrows arched, and he hurried to add, "I didn't say I agreed."

"That's right," Forest said. "So we figured if we got rid of a few, everybody would see how cool the others are."

His brother added, "Then maybe other people would start putting lights in their yards too. You said you'd give them away for free, so we didn't think you'd care."

Thacker looked more perplexed than angry. "Then why did you steal them? Why not come to us and explain?"

Forest scuffed the toe of his shoe on the sidewalk. "We didn't wanna hurt your feelings by telling you people think your lights are ugly."

"'Cause we think they're awesome." Heath pointed at the frog. "'Specially that one."

Thacker aimed a suspicious look at Al. "How do you fit into this? Did you help them?"

"Me? No!" Al shook his head. "They pulled this off all by themselves. I was as much in the dark as everyone else until this afternoon, when I found the missing decorations behind my pond. I wouldn't have known who was responsible except for this."

From his pocket he extracted the scrap he'd found stuck in the tinsel-covered fountain and held it up. A bubblegum wrapper. The same brand the boys had been chewing last Saturday when they helped him decorate.

Heath glared at Forest. "Ain't I always telling you not to litter?"

Forest gave his brother a look full of disgust and then said, "We'd have stashed them somewhere closer, except they're so big we couldn't figure out anyplace they wouldn't get found."

Lulu awarded the boys an admiring smile. "These two snuck out of their house in the mid-

111

dle of the night, picked up a sculpture, and carried it out to Al and Millie's place all by themselves, just so we wouldn't have people upset with us. Isn't that the sweetest thing you've ever heard?"

"Are you gonna call the cops?" Fear drenched the older boy's voice.

"That's why we stopped at only three," Heath said. "'Cause Mama said Mrs. Richardson said Mrs. Thacker said you were gonna call the cops."

Thacker rocked back on his heels, eyeing the culprits. "Weeeeellll, I guess good intentions ought to count for something."

The brothers looked at each other, perplexed.

"That means he's not going to call the police," Al told them.

"But I want the missing pieces returned." Thacker aimed a frown down at them. "And no getting help, either. You took them by yourselves, and you can bring them back by yourselves."

"Only in daylight," Lulu added. "No more climbing out of windows in the dark."

They agreed, and after delivering official apologies and enduring Lulu's kisses on their cheeks, Al loaded them into the backseat of his car. He shut the door and turned to face

Thacker.

"You're going easy on them."

Thacker shrugged. "They're just kids."

"Their mother isn't likely to be so under-standing. Our next stop is the veterinary clinic, so they can confess to her." Al glanced at his watch. "She gets off in ten minutes."

Concern flooded Lulu's face. "I hope she's not too hard on them."

"They need to be punished," Al said. "How else are they going to learn that there are consequences for being dishonest?"

Thacker gave Al a loaded look. "That's a lesson some others I can think of need to learn."

His cheeks burning, Al slid behind the wheel and made his escape.

Chapter Eight

On the morning of the party, Millie awoke long before dawn. By the time the sun came up, she had rolled three dozen ham-and-cheese pinwheels, mixed up the crab salad, prepped the artichoke dip for baking, and created a huge Christmas tree-shaped relish tray.

Eight varieties of cookies were thawing on the dining room table, and the heavenly aroma of chocolate cake wafted from the oven. Christmas carols played softly from the radio, and she hummed along as she filled mini pastry shells with the chicken salad she'd made yesterday. Rufus sat at attention at her feet, his nose twitching and his dark eyes begging for her to have pity and toss him a morsel.

When Albert entered the room, she stopped her task long enough to pour his coffee and refill her own.

"Why didn't you wake me?" He eyed the results of her labor over the rim of his mug. "I could have helped."

"There's still plenty to do." Returning to her chair, she gestured for him to join her at the table. "Drink your coffee, and when you're awake enough to handle a knife, you can slice the salami."

When the last pastry shell had been filled, she slid the tray into the fridge and then crossed that task off of her to-do list. Scanning the page, she fought against an unreasonable stab of nerves. A satisfying number of items had been completed, but she still had over half a page to go before the guests arrived.

A glance at the clock helped to restore her

calm. The party didn't start for another eight hours. The house was spotless, and every room tastefully decorated for the holiday. She'd be ready.

She turned from the counter in time to see Albert pop a thick piece of salami into his mouth.

"What?" He attempted to look innocent. "It was uneven. Would have looked bad on the tray."

"Hmm." Unable to hold the mock frown for more than a few seconds, she crossed the room and kissed his cheek. "Thank you."

"For what?"

"Suggesting this party." Straightening, she glanced at the counter, which was covered with tempting appetizers ready to serve her guests. "It was the perfect thing to get me in the Christmas spirit. Not that I won't still miss Alison," she hurried to add, "but planning for tonight has been fun."

The oddest expression came over his face. It took her a moment to identify, and when she did, she cocked her head. Why did Albert look guilty?

"Is everything okay?" she asked.

He didn't answer at first but continued to slice round slivers of the spicy meat. "Actually, there's some—" At the ringing of her cell phone, his mouth snapped shut.

She glanced at the screen and snatched up the phone. "It's Frieda. I hope she's not calling to tell me she can't come. Hello?"

"You won't believe what she's done now."

Though there was only one person about whom Frieda would call this early on a Saturday, Millie asked, "What who's done?"

"Your *friend*, of course." She made the word sound like an insult. "The decoration queen of Main Street."

Millie winced at the biting sarcasm. "Oh, dear. What is it this time?"

"You've got to see it to believe it. Come down here."

"I can't go anywhere. I'm getting ready for the party." She realized she spoke to dead air. Frieda had hung up.

Albert had stopped slicing to watch her. "What's wrong?"

"Apparently Lulu has taken it upon herself to do some more decorating." Resigned, she unplugged the phone from the charger and slid it into her pocket. "I've been summoned downtown."

He set down the knife. "I'll go with you."

Al parked the car in front of the Whistlestop Café. They got out, and Millie came around to his side. The new display had already drawn a crowd. For a moment they stood, taking in the view.

The decorated Douglas fir, lights off at this hour of the morning, stood in its place of honor at the end of Main Street. From this angle, it could barely be seen behind a huge inflated plastic globe with the words *Merry Christmas* printed inside on the backdrop of a cartoon version of a snowy wonderland. Another globe, slightly smaller, stood to the right of the tree, and yet another to the left. In fact, the entire grassy circle around the tree was full of inflatable globes. A loud hum carried on the chilly morning air above the murmur of voices coming from those assembled, and Al spied fake snow swirling inside the plastic bubbles.

"Oh my." Millie stood transfixed, her hand covering her mouth.

"I definitely see the Thacker touch," he offered, which earned him a sharp look.

Someone in the cluster of onlookers caught

sight of them and broke away from the crowd to stomp in their direction. Frieda. Judging by her stern expression, she wasn't about to deliver praise for the town's new decorations.

"Do you see that?" The woman waved a wild hand behind her as she approached. "Just look what she's done to our town."

Millie put on a forced smile. "They're certainly…big."

A snort blasted from Frieda's nose. "To say the least. There's a snowman on that side." She pointed toward the far side of the tree. "And a Santa on this one. And in the front is a nativity!" Her chest inflated with an outraged intake of breath. "A nativity in a *snow globe*!"

Al ventured a question. "Is that all?"

The woman rounded on him, nostrils flaring. "All? All! Reducing our Savior's birth to a…a…an *air-filled debacle*!"

Actually, Frieda's agitation filled Al with the desire to see the nativity globe and judge for himself. He rarely sided with the opinionated woman, even if she was a business owner.

Another car pulled into the parking lot and came to a halt beside theirs. Jerry and Cindie Selbo emerged, their gazes fixed on the town's new decorations.

"Wow." The mayor approached with his

long-legged gait. "It's eye-catching, I'll give her that."

"How much do you suppose those things cost?" Al asked.

"I saw some at the hardware store last week," Jerry answered. "They were smaller than these, but still four hundred dollars. I can't imagine how much they paid."

"Lulu shops on eBay," Millie offered. "She's really good at finding bargains."

Frieda stepped forward to stand less than a foot in front of Millie, and thrust her face within inches. "I don't care how much of a bargain she got, they're gaudy and tacky and we won't stand for it. You've got to do something!"

Anger stirred Al to action. He strode forward and thrust himself between his beloved and her attacker. "Why does Millie have to do anything? She's not the Main Street Manager. We don't even own a business in town, not yet. And not on Main Street. If you don't like it, *you* do something about it."

"No!" Placing a hand on his shoulder, Millie stepped around him. "Lulu is only trying to do a good job. She loves serving the town, and honestly, who else would be willing to do her job for free?"

A glance at Mayor Selbo and Frieda, who

failed to meet anyone's eye at the moment, provided the answer. No one.

"Let me talk to her. I'll get her to see reason." Millie squared her shoulders, earning even more of Al's respect. What a woman he'd married! "But not today. I have too much going on. After church tomorrow I'll sit down with her and have a heart-to-heart."

Frieda's eyes narrowed, while Jerry and Cindie exchanged a glance. Then all three nodded.

"But tomorrow night is it," Frieda warned. "After that, I'll take a knife to the things."

She strode off, stomping in the direction of the Freckled Frog like an offended drill sergeant.

When she was out of earshot, Al spoke to no one in particular. "I want to see that nativity."

He sauntered toward the expanding crowd, aware that Millie and the Selbos fell in step behind him. The four circled the clearing. On one side a happy inflatable snowman, complete with black top hat and corncob pipe, perched amid a flurry of white flakes. A pair of children stood with their faces plastered to the bubble, mesmerized by the snowstorm inside the globe. Their parents stood behind them, snapping pictures. Lucy Cardwell and Tuesday Love had placed themselves in front of the nativity globe.

Tuesday grinned at their approach. "I just *love* Snoopy. *A Charlie Brown Christmas* has been one of my favorite holiday shows since I was a kid."

Sure enough, the globe featured the characters from the beloved comic strip. Above the plastic bubble, Sally in angel garb smiled down at Charlie, Lucy, and Snoopy, all gazing into a manger.

"I think it's cute," Cindie commented. At a sharp glance from the owner of Cardwell Drugstore, she amended the comment. "Of course, it doesn't fit here, but it's a nice yard decoration for someone who likes this sort of thing."

More people joined them, and Al nodded at those he recognized. Creekers gathering for their traditional Saturday morning coffee at the drugstore's soda fountain detoured to get a look at the new decorations.

"Woudja lookit that?" Norman Pilkington's voice rose above the others. "Hit's Santy Clause in this 'un."

Little Norm called from the other side. "Frosty's over here, Pa."

Al and Millie had done the full circuit and halted in front of the biggest bubble, the one with the backdrop.

"What's this supposed to be?" Al cocked his

head and eyed the vacant space in front of the winter scene. "It looks empty."

Millie opened her mouth to answer, but at that moment some people approached. The man held his cell phone toward Al. "Would you get our picture?"

After instructing Al to "just press that dot," he ushered his family through a hidden door in the backdrop. The four stood in the empty space, characters in their own snow globe scene. The children shouted, "Cheese!" and Al pressed the button. Then he backed up a few steps. From this angle, the camera lens could capture the entire west side of Main Street, with all the wreaths and storefront decorations. He snapped several more shots.

Millie stood beside him, taking in the view. "At night, when the wreath lights are on, that could be a really nice picture."

The family trooped out, thanked Al, and then stepped aside to view the pictures he'd snapped. The children giggled, and the parents wore broad smiles as they waved goodbye and continued toward the Whistlestop, apparently for breakfast.

The Selbos approached, and Jerry stood with his hands planted on his hips, head cocked, looking at the display. "You know, it's not bad.

I kind of like it."

Al's lips twitched. "Don't let Frieda hear you say that."

Cindie nodded agreement. "Decorations are like art. Some people like landscapes, some like nouveau, some like impressionist. There's a place for everything."

"That's true." Millie glanced down the street toward the Freckled Frog. "But I'm afraid I agree with Frieda. Main Street isn't the place for this kind of decoration." Her eyes brightened. "Maybe we could suggest that we move these somewhere. The front of the elementary school, maybe."

Jerry appeared to consider and then shrugged. "I'm not sure Lulu will go for it, but you can try." Then he brightened. "We're looking forward to the party tonight."

"Can we bring anything?" Cindie asked.
"Don't you dare." Millie glanced up at the sky. "But you might say a prayer that the storm holds off."

The weather forecast notwithstanding, Millie's house filled with party guests. A tasteful display of glowing garland, twinkling shrubs, and peppermint-wrapped columns on the front porch welcomed everyone. She conducted countless tours of the upstairs bedrooms, revealing each one with pride. A color-draped evergreen twinkled in the Bo Peep room, and what else could she have put in the Little Boy Blue room but a silver tree with blue lights? The crowning glory of the house stood in the entry hall, a ten-foot Colorado blue spruce glowing with all the colors of the rainbow, an ornament dangling from every branch.

The Wainright boys, doing penance with serious expressions and matching red bow ties, accepted people's coats and hung them on rented coatracks in the hallway. Fern, hired for the occasion to ensure that no tray on the dining room table ever went empty, carried out her duties with a solemn competency that impressed Millie no end.

"Oh my goodness, would you look at that!" Tuesday Love, who arrived decked out in a faux fur jacket which she refused to relinquish, exclaimed over the elaborate display of treats. "Why, it's like Santa himself came to visit."

Millie drifted from one cluster of guests to

another, chatting and tasting and gracefully accepting accolades for the elaborate display and scrumptious food.

Susan and Justin arrived, he in a suit and she sporting a little black dress that Millie might have worn three decades ago.

"The house looks beautiful," Susan told her.

"And you look lovely, dear." Millie turned to Justin. "I made your favorite corn bread, but I suggest you hurry. It's going fast."

His eyes lit. "You made broccoli corn bread?"

Dismay overtook Susan's features. "Corn bread with *broccoli* in it? Really?"

"Honest, hon, it's the best thing you've ever tasted." Justin grabbed her by the hand and tugged her toward the dining room.

Albert, looking extremely handsome in his gray suit and red silk tie, emerged from the parlor. "Have you met Ansel Crowder? Nice guy."

Millie peeked past him and spied Alice smiling shyly at the man she'd brought as her guest. Lately she had looked tired and careworn, but tonight the deep lines on her face had disappeared. Good. She deserved an evening of fun.

"It's going well, don't you think?" Millie whispered to Albert.

"Absolutely." He slipped an arm around her waist and planted a kiss on her cheek. "You've outdone yourself."

The front door was thrown open, and the Thackers made their entrance. Really, that was the only way to describe the way they strode into the house, arm in arm, decked out in matching Christmas sweaters. Millie's jaw went slack, completely at a loss for words to describe the 3D blinking trees plastered across their chests, complete with tinsel and strands of lights that encircled their necks.

Franklin paused on the threshold and shouted, "Merry *Honk*mas, fellow geese." He proceeded to flap his elbows and shout, "Honk, honk, honk" to the tune of "Jingle Bells," while Lulu erupted in peals of laughter that echoed up the staircase and into the far reaches of the house. In the dining room, Violet stopped her conversation with Doris to give an expansive eye roll.

"Merry Christmas." Millie greeted Lulu with a cautious hug. "I don't want to knock anything off of your, uh, tree."

"Don't worry." Lulu dismissed the concern with a wave. "I used so much hot glue attaching all these do-dads they're not going anywhere."

Albert shook hands with Franklin, and closed the door against a biting wind.

Lulu's wide lips stretched into a gigantic

smile. "Well? Have you been downtown to-day?"

"Actually, yes. I saw the new decorations this morning."

"They look great, don't they? Just wait till you see them all lit up at night." She hooked an arm through Franklin's. "We took a lesson from those cute little boys and did the work in the middle of the night so people would wake up to a surprise this morning. Then we had to sleep half the day to catch up." She gave a wide yawn. "I'm not as young as I used to be."

"We drove down Main Street on the way here," Franklin said, "but nobody much was around. Figured they were probably all here." He craned his neck to scan the guests. "Looks like we were right."

Millie gestured graciously toward the dining room. "Go on inside and help yourself to food."

"First things first. Lookie here." From a large bag Lulu produced a gift-wrapped box. "I brought you something."

Millie took the package thrust at her. "But the invitations said no gifts. This party is for fun, not presents."

"It's not for the party, honey." Her teeth appeared in the midst of a wide grin. "It's 'cause you're my friend. Go ahead. Open it."

How could one decline such a sweet gesture? As she slid a fingernail beneath the tape, Millie wracked her brain for something to give Lulu in return. Thank goodness there were still two weeks before Christmas. A small crowd gathered around them as she pulled the last of the paper off the box and handed it to Albert.

Lulu spread her generous smile around the watchers. "I made it with my own hands. It's as unique as Millie herself."

With those words, Millie's nerves began to jitter. Apprehension high, she lifted the top off the box.

A gasp rose from the assembled.

"Oh my." Her long-deceased mother's voice whispered in her ear. *If you can't say anything nice...* But when receiving a gift, one *must* reply. "It's..." She gulped, her mind as empty as a vacuum. Finally, she managed to choke out, "It's a sweater with a pair of snowmen."

"Aren't they adorable?" Lulu snatched the garment from the box and held it up for everyone to see. The snowmen were strategically placed so that their hats climbed up the sweater's shoulders. "Those eyes are made outta real coal, and their mouths are little black buttons. And see how that gold tinsel at the cuffs matches the decoration on their hats?"

Virginia Smith

"The feathers were my idea." Franklin's chest puffed out. "Adds a nice touch, don't you think?"

Millie extended a finger to touch the bright green feather boa that encircled the sweater's hem and also covered the snowmen's hats. But she could not tear her gaze from the giant orange carrots. They protruded at least six inches. Two of them. One on each side.

"I…" She gulped and forced a smile. "Thank you, Lulu. This is the most unique gift I have ever received."

An approving titter rose from the watchers, along with a snort from somewhere behind her. Violet, no doubt. Millie ignored her.

"You're welcome." Lulu grinned at her husband. "And since we're all here, I have an announcement."

Franklin's eyes went round. He shook his head. "No, Sugar Lips. Now's not the time."

"What better time?" Lulu spread her arms wide to indicate the party guests. "So many of our Goose Creek friends are here."

The look Franklin cast toward Albert contained a panicky tinge that Millie had never seen the normally confident—and somewhat clueless—man wear.

"Well, now you've got us curious," said Justin.

"That's right," Cindie added. "You can't leave us hanging."

Franklin continued to shake his head, and he even extended a hand toward his wife's face as if to muzzle her. Lulu assumed a proud stance, her long neck stretched to its fullest length.

"My Frankie's moving up in the world. He just got a big promotion at work. You're looking at the new Manager of Software Development."

"What?" Albert's shout held an edge of outrage that gave it enough volume to echo up the stairs.

Surprised, Millie turned in time to see him stride across the hardwood floor and come to a stop in front of Franklin. "They fired me and then promoted *you*?"

The words rang in a sudden silence like Christmas bells on a snowy morning.

Al's gut burned as if he'd gulped a gallon of battery acid. The stares of his friends and neighbors pressed on him from all sides, but they were nothing to the laser beams coming from Millie's eyes. One by one the guests slipped away, congregating in the dining room or parlor or anywhere away from the uncomfortable silence of the entry hall.

Lulu watched them go, confusion clear on her face. "What's wrong? Why isn't anybody congratulating you, Honey Bun?"

Thacker gave her a look that clearly said *not now,* and stepped toward Al. "I'm sorry, Bert. It came as a surprise to me too. But what was I gonna do, turn it down because they let my buddy go?"

Al barely heard him. Instead, his entire attention was fixed on his beloved wife, whose face bore an alarming blend of anger and injury. Being one of the most intelligent women he knew, no doubt her brain was sifting through a dozen or so tidbits from the past two weeks. Phone calls from his cell instead of the office. Research trips to the library. An increase in the gasoline budget, because he'd spent far more time driving than usual. Even this party. No doubt the reason behind his suggestion was dawning on her at this moment.

She uttered only one word. "When?"

He considered lying, but only for a second. He was tired of lying. And no matter how he'd convinced himself that he had not actually uttered a lie, deceit was a form of lying. Lies had a way of expanding and multiplying. Utter a lie, and before you knew it, you'd told five others to cover the first.

He hung his head. "The Friday before Thanksgiving."

Fiery red splotches erupted on her face, but she made no reply. Instead she gave a single nod, turned, and stomped down the hallway in the direction of the kitchen.

Lulu stared after her for a moment, and then she rounded on him. "Do you mean to say you got fired more than three weeks ago and you never told your wife?"

"Now, Sugar Lips." Thacker took her by the arm and pulled her back. "The man had his reasons. He's been putting together a plan, applying for jobs and learning new skills and such."

Her mouth gaped open to its full, not-inconsiderable size. "You *knew*? All this time you knew and didn't tell me?"

Thacker took a long-legged step back, his hands raised in a posture of self-defense and cast a desperate glance toward Al. "He swore me to secrecy."

Shoulders slumped, Al told Lulu, "It's not his fault. The blame is all mine. I just wanted some time." He glanced down the hallway to where Millie had disappeared.

Lulu followed his gaze. "I think your time is up." She placed a hand on his back and shoved him toward the kitchen.

Moving like a condemned man, Al scuffed his shoes all the way down the hall. Heath and Forest, seated on the carpenter's bench near the coat racks, raised sympathetic glances from their video games as he passed.

He found Millie in the kitchen with Violet. Their whispered conversation fell silent when he entered, and Millie presented her back to him. Violet awarded him a tight-lipped scowl.

"May we have a minute alone?" he asked.

As she slipped by him, she said, "The cat's out of the bag now. Your name is mud. You'd best come clean and no bones about it."

A part of his mind admired her ability to use four appropriate clichés at once, but he had no energy to waste on her. The woman in front of him whose spine appeared stiffer than a steel rod commanded all his attention.

Until a few minutes ago, his plan to delay telling Millie he'd lost his job didn't seem so bad. He'd been so sure something better would come along. For weeks he'd entertained visions of sitting her down and saying, "J&J let me go, but don't worry. I found a better job *here.*" In retrospect, his actions looked far more nefarious, even loathsome, than they had at the time.

What could he say to make this right? A mere apology wouldn't cut it this time. Major groveling was definitely in order.

"Millie—"

She whirled on him, anger sparking from her eyes and a large knife shining in her hand. "Don't talk to me."

He gulped. "But I—"

"I mean it, Albert. This is not the time." Returning to the counter, she tackled a stack of celery with vicious slices.

At times like this, a wise man had only one recourse. Moving as silently as he could, Al backed out of the kitchen and slunk into his private den, where he planned to spend the rest of the evening praying for mercy.

Broccoli Corn Bread

1 box (10 ounces) frozen chopped broccoli

1 large onion, diced

1 stick butter

1 small box corn bread mix, such as Jiffy

3 eggs (may use ³/₄ cup of egg substitute)

1 cup low-fat or fat-free cottage cheese

Preheat oven to 350°. Grease a 9-inch round cake pan or an 8 x 8-inch square baking dish. Cook broccoli according to directions on package; drain well. Sauté onion in butter until tender and stir into broccoli. In a second bowl, combine eggs and cottage cheese, and then stir in corn bread mix. Add broccoli mixture and stir until combined. Pour into prepared pan and bake for 35 minutes. Cool slightly. Cut into wedges or squares and serve warm with butter.

Chapter Nine

The evening felt as if it lasted weeks for Millie. Albert's absence was noticed by everyone and commented on by no one, which made the whole situation a hundred times more embarrassing. Millie smiled and chatted, accepting congratulations on the food and the house and her hostessing skills, all the while wrestling with the infuriating truth: Her husband had lied to her. Not a simple white lie. A big, ugly, black lie that he'd kept up for weeks.

As the food dwindled and the guests began to bid her goodbye, anger gave way to despair. How could he keep something huge like this from her? They were best friends, partners in life, joined together as one thirty-eight years ago. How many lies had he told and not been caught? How much of their relationship, which she'd always thought was based on truth, was a lie?

Finally, only a handful of people remained. Susan and Justin circled the house picking up napkins and scraping leftover scraps into garbage bags. Lulu carried trays and bowls from the dining room to the kitchen, where Violet busily stuffed leftovers into plastic storage bags and managed to find room for them in the refrigerator.

Millie was in the parlor wiping icing off of a marble end table when Franklin entered. She glanced up, noted his long face, and focused on her task.

"Are you mad at me too?" he asked.

Truthfully, she was. A little. He was an accomplice in Albert's deception. But being angry with an outsider would serve no purpose. "Of course not."

"You ought to be. I would be." He flopped down onto the settee. "Lulu is furious. Says you're her best friend in the whole world, and I ought to be horsewhipped for helping Bert hurt you."

"A horsewhip." She managed a smile. "There's an idea."

He indulged in a low chuckle, nothing like his typical snorting guffaw, and then he became serious. "Don't be too hard on him. He's been through a lot these last few weeks."

The icing gone, Millie folded the damp dishrag. "What do you mean?"

"For one, he was the only guy they got rid of. They kept everybody else and even hired two new programmers. That's hard for a man to take."

A pinprick of sympathy stabbed through her anger. "Why did they get rid of him? Did he do something wrong?"

"Of course not!" Franklin leaned forward to plant his forearms on his thighs. "We're phasing out the system he worked on and getting a new one. In the computer industry, you've got to stay on top of changes in technology. Bert hasn't. Besides, he's…" He pursed his lips, and then continued in an apologetic tone. "Well, he's getting on up there, you know? He was the oldest guy in the whole department. After decades of pay raises, he made too much money."

The meaning sank in, and Millie dropped onto the cushion beside Franklin. They fired Albert because he was old. How embarrassing that must have been for him. And how humiliating.

"Why didn't he tell me?"

She voiced the question foremost in her mind, not really expecting an answer. But Franklin did.

"He didn't say, but I've thought about it a lot, and I think I know the reason." He glanced toward the doorway, and then he leaned closer to speak in a low voice. "My Sugar Lips thinks I'm a man's man, you know? Strong. In charge." He threw his chest out. "Virile, if you get my meaning."

She ignored the last adjective but did take his meaning. "Albert doesn't want me to think he's old and worthless."

"It's only a guess, but that's what I'd be worried about if I were in his place."

Millie was still considering that when the object of the conversation entered the room. He wore a hang-dog expression that hurt her more than any deceit. Her Albert should never think himself worthless.

"Just in case anyone wants to know, the storm has arrived," he announced. "It's sleeting now, and the Weather Channel says it's going to be pretty bad."

Thacker launched himself off the settee. "We'd better get home."

In the hallway they found Lulu, Violet, Susan, and Justin donning their coats.

Lulu caught sight of Franklin. "Frankie, we're gonna give Violet a ride home since we've got four-wheel drive."

Violet hugged Millie goodbye. "I'll get my car tomorrow."

"It was a great party," Susan told her as she and Justin left.

Millie stood on the deep front porch, shivering in the frigid wind, and watched the last of her guests make their way carefully across the slush-covered sidewalk, hunching against the falling sleet. She lifted a hand in farewell as their taillights retreated down the long driveway.

Then she turned to Albert. "We need to talk." He nodded, his posture sagging, and followed her into the house.

They sat in the parlor. Al perched on the edge of one of the wing chairs and stared morosely into the murky liquid inside his mug.

Curled up on the settee, Millie blew a cloud of steam from her teacup and took a sip. "I wish you'd trusted me enough to tell me."

"I do trust you," he rushed to assure her, and then he dropped his gaze again. "It wasn't a matter of trust. It was…"

"You were afraid I would think less of you if you got fired?"

He winced. The words still stung. "Not so much you. It was more about me." Selfish words, and he felt like a heel saying them, but they were the truth. "I guess the blow to my ego was more than I could handle, and I reacted poorly." He raised his eyes to catch her in a direct look. "I'm sorry. I should have told you when it happened. I just kept thinking I'd find another job, and then the news wouldn't seem as bad."

"It's not so bad anyway." She put on a brave smile. "We'll make it. The house has taken a lot of our savings, but we still have some. I'm sure if I explain the situation to Susan and Alice, I can go back to five days a week at the veterinary clinic."

With a start, Al realized she knew none of the details. How could she, when he'd held this so closely to his chest? "You don't have to do that. We have plenty of money. They wrote me a check for seventy-five weeks' worth of pay, plus we still have insurance coverage."

Her jaw dropped. "Why would they fire someone and then treat them so well?"

"It's an early retirement package. They made sure I didn't lose anything by accepting."

She sat up. "Are you saying you weren't fired? You were retired?"

He nodded, affirming the glum truth.

"But Albert, that's *good* news. We should be celebrating." A broad grin erupted, and a pair of adorable dimples put in an appearance. "You're retired! That means I can retire too. We can open the B&B, and go to the beach in your RV, and do all the things we've planned."

When he didn't join with her enthusiasm, she peered more closely at him. "That's the problem, isn't it?" A note of hurt crept into her tone. "You didn't tell me because you don't want to open the B&B."

He wanted to deny it simply to spare her feelings, but he was through with deception. "That was part of it," he admitted. "I kept trying to picture myself carrying luggage and taking orders from my wife. It wasn't an appealing prospect."

"I...see." Tears glimmered in her eyes, and Al's chest tightened.

"Not at first, anyway." He extended a hand across the distance. "But the past few days getting ready for this party, we were doing it *together.* I realized I enjoyed working with you."

A hesitant smile returned. She reached out and took his hand. "I've enjoyed it too."

Al squeezed. "Maybe it won't be so bad, having my wife be the boss."

"Not the boss," she corrected. "We're partners. We'll do it together." She drew in a breath. "Besides, there's no rush. We don't have to open the business now. Let's take some time and enjoy our retirement first."

Gazing at the woman he had loved for more than half his life, Al's heart swelled to fill his chest. He didn't deserve her. For some inexplicable reason, God had given her to him anyway.

"I'm so sorry I didn't tell you right away. What a jerk I've been. Will you forgive me?"

Instead of answering, she set her tea on the side table and, without releasing his hand, left the settee and slid onto his lap. "Tell you what." She slipped an arm around his neck and pulled his head toward hers. "I'll let you earn your way back into my good graces."

Her kiss was as passionate as a newlywed's. Al applied his efforts toward returning it with the energy of a man half his age.

Millie awoke to the sound of someone pounding on the front door.

"Huh?" Al lifted his head off the pillow. "Wazzit?"

"I think someone's here." She sat up in bed, yawning, and glanced at the clock on the night stand. Eight thirty! A grin stole across her lips. Ah, the luxury of retirement. She would have slid back beneath the sheets and cuddled next to her husband, but the banging returned.

"Who in the world would show up at this hour of the morning?" Al got out of bed, grumbling like an old bear.

"I don't know, but they're certainly insistent."

Millie threw on her bathrobe and slid her feet into her slippers. She followed Albert down the hallway, her hand covering another yawn.

Rufus joined them, barking a belated alarm at the same moment the sound of her cell phone ringing in the kitchen reached her.

Al threw open the door, and when they caught sight of the couple standing on the porch his scowl dissolved. "Thacker, what are you doing here?"

Lulu lowered her cell phone from her ear, and Millie's went silent. "We've been calling for twenty minutes. Don't you answer your phone?"

"I must have left it in the other room last night." Millie exchanged a private smile with Albert before taking in the view before them. "Oh my!"

The anticipated storm had blown through town and left a shimmering winter scene in its wake. The sun shone with such ferocity that she had to shield her eyes. Every tree branch, every individual blade of grass, was coated with a glittering sheen of ice. The lawn stretched out before her, gleaming like a field of crystals. Her eyes dazzled by the beauty, Millie could only stare in wonder.

"Oh good gravy. Look at that."

She followed the direction where Albert pointed. One of the huge trees that bordered their property had splintered down the center, and half of the trunk lay across the drive. The ice-laden branches of the blue spruce at the corner of the house drooped dangerously low to the ground.

"Power lines are down all over," Franklin told them. "You're lucky yours are underground. And I hate to tell you, buddy, but your RV wasn't so lucky."

"What?" Albert darted into the house and through the back door, Millie and the Thackers on his heels and Rufus darting between his legs, barking like a crazed creature. From the veranda they had an unimpeded view of Albert's motorhome, a huge tree branch lying across the front. The shards that glittered in the sunlight here were not ice, but pieces of the shattered windshield.

Millie slipped an arm around his waist. "Don't worry. That's what insurance is for."

"At least you *have* insurance." Lulu's nasally whine grated more irritatingly than usual. "We can't say the same."

"Oh no." Millie reached toward her. "Was your house damaged?"

"Not the house." Franklin cast a sorrowful look at his wife. "The snow globes."

"They're in shreds," Lulu moaned. "Frieda called this morning, and we hurried right down there. Nothing left but piles of colored plastic. Ice sliced through them like daggers from heaven."

No doubt Frieda would say daggers falling from the sky were an answer to prayer. Millie covered her mouth to hide a chuckle that would offend her friend.

"Maybe they can be repaired," Albert said. "We'll help if we can."

"Thanks." Lulu heaved a sigh. "But I'm taking this as a sign. Let the town stick with white lights and wreaths. At least this year."

Millie gave her a sympathetic smile. "I think that's a good decision. Come on inside. I'll put on some coffee, and you can join us for a breakfast of party leftovers."

Franklin gazed between the two of them. "You two patch things up?" He glanced quickly at Lulu. "No pun intended."

Millie and Albert exchanged another smile. "Everything's fine in the Richardson house."

Arm in arm, they led their friends inside.

Chapter Ten

"Grammy! Pawpaw! Wake up! It's Christmas!"

Al awoke to the weight of six-year-old Abby bouncing on his chest. William, seven, leapfrogged onto his pillow, dangerously close to his head, while little Lionel ran around the bed screeching a nearly unintelligible three-year-old version of, "Santa came! Santa came!"

Millie popped up with a sixty-watt smile, as if she had not been awake just three hours before helping build a princess castle out of Legos.

"Merry Christmas!" she shouted in a singsong voice while grabbing for Lionel and dragging him onto the bed.

The ensuing moments were spent in a happy roly-poly that ended in a pillow fight, during which Al slid out of bed to stand in a safe corner to officiate and Millie slipped from the room.

"Here, now!" Al pointed at William. "No clobbering kids less than half your age." When they all stopped to look at him, he crouched, grinning. "Not when I can get to them first!" He charged, grasped Lionel up and tossed him onto the bed. The toddler bounced, giggling, while William smashed Al in the head with his own pillow.

"All right, kids." A stern voice invaded their fun, and Al looked up to see his son, Doug, standing in the doorway with his hands planted on his hips. "Don't torture Pawpaw anymore. We have presents to open."

When the kids would have dashed past him, Al hopped to his feet. "Wait!"

Everyone screeched to a halt.

"You know the rules." He gathered his face into a mock-serious frown. "No opening presents until I've had my breakfast."

"Oh, Pawpaw!" Abby collapsed dramatically on the floor. "That'll take *forever*."

"How about this?" Millie appeared behind Doug holding a steaming Grinch-shaped mug. "Let Pawpaw have a sip of coffee first, and *then* we'll open presents."

"Well." Al heaved a long-suffering sigh. "I *suppose* that'll be okay."

Screeching their delight, the kids ran past the adults toward the parlor, where Al knew their mothers waited, video cameras ready to capture those first few moments of enchantment when the children spied their gifts.

The adults followed at a slightly less enthusiastic pace and arrived in time to see the kids dive for the tree.

In the far corner, David tapped away on a laptop. He turned with a wide smile. "I've got them!"

Millie left Al's side and rushed to the computer, where Alison's face filled the screen.

"Merry Christmas, darling! And sweet Melody! Merry first Christmas! Grammy loves you."

Tears sparkled in his wife's eyes, and Al

blinked away a few of his own.

"Merry Christmas, Daddy," his little girl said from thousands of miles away.

He managed to ease out a "Merry Christmas, baby" without embarrassing himself.

As it happened every year, the kids ripped through their gifts in record time, barely stopping to admire one before reaching for the next. Al didn't mind in the least. Later on, when the excitement died down, William would appreciate the chemistry set he'd selected, and Abby would cuddle her new baby doll like a miniature mother. Lionel, in typical single-minded fashion, had to be coaxed to leave one gift and move on to the next.

When the tree—not the giant, decorative one in the entry hall but the smaller one in the cozier parlor—had been stripped bare of gifts, a sort of calm descended upon the family. Millie refilled the adults' coffee mugs, all except Sarah, who was eschewing coffee for the duration of her pregnancy, and they sat back to watch the kids play with their new toys. On the laptop monitor, Alison rocked baby Melody, while Nick gazed at the pair with love shining in his eyes that Al recognized and gloried in.

"Well, Dad?" Alison's voice crackled through the speakers. "Are you going to do it or not?"

Millie, who was helping Abby dress a Barbie doll in a princess outfit, fixed him with a curious glance. "Do what, Albert?"

"Oh, just this." He heaved himself out of his chair and strode to the tree. "Looks like there's one more present we haven't opened." He plucked a long envelope from its hiding place in the bows of the tree. Working hard to conceal his grin, he held it at arm's length and squinted at the writing. "Looks like it's for you, Millie."

"For me?" She smiled down at Abby. "I wonder who it's from."

The little girl ventured a guess. "Santa?"

"Maybe." Millie took the envelope from his hands and examined it. "Hmm. The handwriting looks familiar. More like Pawpaw's than Santa's."

She held his gaze as her fingers pried open the flap. Then she looked down. Al's breath caught in his chest. Though he knew she would love the gift, an odd tension built in his stomach as he awaited her reaction.

Wonder dawned on her face. She lifted eyes full of questions. "We're going to Italy?"

Grinning, he nodded. "For a whole month. We leave in three weeks."

While their children and grandchildren filled

the air with cheers, Millie launched herself out of the chair and into his arms. Sobbing so hard she could barely speak, she managed to choke, "Oh, Albert, this is the best gift ever."

Wrapping her into a hug, Al held her close. Though her happiness filled him with joy, she was wrong. The best gift ever was right here in his arms.

Acknowledgements

I'm deeply grateful to several people for helping me tell this story. First, I will never be able to find adequate words to express my appreciation to Kathleen Kerr, my Harvest House editor, for the Tales from the Goose Creek B&B series. Her belief in these stories, and in my ability to tell them, inspires and humbles me.

Huge thanks to my longtime friend Becky Hodge for talking with me about retirement packages and pension plans. And for introducing me to a really cool restaurant.

Normally when I include a recipe in a book, I find a base to start with and then tweak it so it becomes my own. The broccoli corn bread recipe in this book came from Carolyn Hawkins, a dear lady who has gained regional fame and notoriety because of her recipe. How could I change perfection? (Here's a secret she told me: Real butter makes all the difference!) Thanks so much, Carolyn.

Once more I want to thank my friends Jerry

and Cindie Selbo for allowing me to use their names for my fictitious characters. Cindie (the real one) does have a lovely singing voice, which is why I thought the fictional Cindie should lead the town's Christmas carols.

Above all I must thank the most important Person in my life — Jesus, the true inspiration behind every story I write.

Soli Deo Gloria

Tales from the Goose Creek B&B

Can't wait to hear all the news from Goose Creek? Read the rest of the story in Virginia Smith's acclaimed series **Tales from the Goose Creek B&B**.

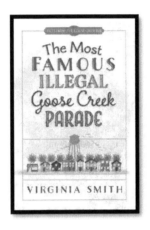

In this first book of the Tales from the Goose Creek B&B, you'll fall in love with a small town that feels like coming home. Its quirky characters and their many shenanigans will make you laugh out loud as they touch a place in your heart.

Even though retirement is still three years away, Al Richardson is counting the days. He anticipates many enjoyable years in which every day feels like Saturday. But Al's wife, Millie, has different plans for their retirement. When she learns that a Victorian-era home is up for sale, Millie launches a full-blown campaign to convince Al that God's plan for them is to turn that house into a B&B.

But a B&B won't be the only change for the small Kentucky town. A new veterinarian has hung up her shingle, but she has only one patient—the smelly dog belonging to her part-time receptionist. And sides are being taken in the issue of the water tower, which needs a new coat of paint…but no one can agree who should paint it.

The situation is coming to a head. Who could have imagined a town protest over a water tower? And who would believe it could culminate in an illegal parade?

Things are finally starting to fall into a steady rhythm in the small town of Goose Creek, Kentucky. Millie Richardson is hard at work renovating a drafty Victorian house into a B&B. Her husband, Al, is busy writing checks for the renovations. And the new vet, Susan, has finally found acceptance from the town—not to mention a hunky new boyfriend, Justin.

But things never stay quiet for long in Goose Creek. The inner-county softball game is coming up, and Millie volunteers Al as team manager. But the softball team is a disaster. If they're not going to embarrass themselves in front of the whole of Franklin County, Al needs Justin to play. But Justin lives just outside the city limits, and the rules say that players must live in town.

As if that weren't enough to keep the town

gossips busy, a massage therapist has come to town and opened up shop. Imagine—a massage parlor!—in Goose Creek! No decent Creeker will stand for it.

It's up to Al and Millie—again—to save the day.

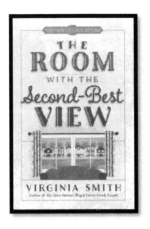

Excitement is in the air in Goose Creek, Kentucky, as the small town prepares to celebrate its 150th anniversary and the veterinarian's upcoming wedding. But trouble is brewing in this provincial paradise...

Al Richardson agreed to open a B&B with his wife after his retirement in two years, but Millie secretly invites some guests to stay for the wedding. She plans to be the most gracious Southern hostess—until a tumble down the stairs leaves her unprepared for their quirky and cantankerous first guest.

Meanwhile, the town's anniversary plans are in a state of chaos as the celebration committee scrambles to raise the necessary funds—an effort spearheaded by a "newcomer," which ruffles the townsfolks' feathers.

Goose Creek has lasted 150 years. Can it survive the next month?

This novella is the perfect introduction to bestselling author Virginia Smith's latest series, Tales from the Goose Creek B&B. Set in the years before the Richardsons launch their bed and breakfast scheme, the quirky residents of the small Kentucky town are all in a tizzy over the upcoming Fall Festival. Alison, Al and Millie's headstrong daughter, astounds everyone with the news that she's getting married—in three weeks—to a Colombian! As her parents frantically try to stop the nuptials, Dr. Horatio, Goose Creek's beloved veterinarian, is determined to solve the mystery of the six-toed kittens that have been popping up all over town.

This charming prequel will make you laugh out loud, fall in love with the delightful residents of Goose Creek, and remind you why you love reading.

Read More from Virginia Smith

TALES FROM THE GOOSE CREEK B & B
Dr. Horatio vs. the Six-Toed Cat
(prequel novella)
The Most Famous Illegal Goose Creek Parade
Renovating the Richardsons
The Room with the Second-Best View
A Goose Creek Christmas
(holiday novella)

THE MEN OF LANCASTER COUNTY
The Amish Widower

Books by Lori Copeland
and Virginia Smith

THE AMISH OF APPLE GROVE
"A Home in the West"
(free short story e-romance prequel)
The Heart's Frontier
A Plain and Simple Heart
A Cowboy at Heart
SEATTLE BRIDES
A Bride for Noah
Rainy Day Dreams

About the Author

Virginia Smith is the bestselling author of more than thirty novels (and counting). Her books have received numerous awards, including two Holt Medallion Awards of Merit. An avid reader with eclectic tastes in fiction, Ginny writes in a variety of styles, from lighthearted relationship stories to breath-snatching suspense. Visit her at
www .VirginiaSmith.org.

66013738R00104

Made in the USA
Charleston, SC
08 January 2017